PRAISE FOR *THE WINTER PRINCE*

"A first novel that compares honorably with Sutcliff's books in its lyrical evocation of Arthur's Britain and is also akin to Napoli's *The Magic Circle* in its contemporary reworking of legendary figures—particularly women. Omitting Merlin and Lancelot, Wein incorporates Welsh lore and names in her story: at Artos's Camlann are his queen, Ginevra, and his three children: twins Goewin and sickly Lleu, Artos's legitimate heir, and their older half-brother Medraut (Mordred), whose narrative is addressed to beautiful, dangerous Morgause—Artos's sister and Medraut's mother—a cruel fascinating woman whose gentle hands more often harm than heal. Conniving to make Medraut Artos's heir, she torments Lleu with poisons, while Medraut—a gifted, richly complex young man whose deep ambivalence about Lleu governs the story— heals and taunts him, teaches, admires, and envies him and finally takes the lad hostage at Morgause's behest. Lleu, coming into his real strengths, turns tables on his captor; their journey home is one of self-realization and reconciliation—themes emblemized, earlier, in solstice celebration when the "Winter Prince"— the Old Year's son—enables the New Year's birth. The metamorphosis of the relationships is both dynamic and subtle, and Wein's chosen voice is intriguing, since there's no setting for the telling—is Medraut still compelled, even when his loyalties have shifted, to explain himself to Morgause? Goewin, who's as able as her brothers and empathizes with her aunt's thwarted ambition, may have a tale of her own. A mesmerizing, splendidly imagined debut."   —*Kirkus*

The Winter Prince

Elizabeth E. Wein

THE WINTER PRINCE

This is a work of fiction. All the characters and events portrayed in this book are fictional, and any resemblance to real people or incidents is purely coincidental.

Copyright © 1993 by Elizabeth E. Wein

A Baen Book

Baen Publishing Enterprises
P.O. Box 1403
Riverdale, NY 10471

ISBN: 0-671-87621-X

Cover art by Darrell K. Sweet

First Baen printing, September 1994

Library of Congress Cataloging-in-Publication Data
Wein, Elizabeth
The Winter Prince / Elizabeth Wein
p. cm.
1. Mordred (Legendary character)—Juvenile Fiction.
2. Arthurian romances. [1. Mordred (Legendary character)—
Fiction. 2. Arthur, King—Fiction. 3. Brothers—Fiction.] I. title.
PZ7.W4358Wi   1993
[Fic]—dc20   91-39129

Distributed by
SIMON & SCHUSTER
1230 Avenue of the Americas
New York, NY 10020

Printed in the United States of America

The Winter Prince

Thou, Nature, art my goddess; to thy law
My services are bound.

—KING LEAR act 1, scene 2

Contents

Prologue

He sat on the floor before the hearth with his knees against his chin, the flames at his back, and warily watched his father's face. His own face was in shadow, and though the April night was too warm for him to be so close to the fire, he did not move away. He did not want his father to see his face; the shadows made him feel safe.

He was an odd, adult child: thin but with a carefully controlled grace, with blank, unreadable, dark blue eyes and hair so pale it sometimes seemed white. His appearance unnerved people; this gave him uncanny strength at times, though not now. He had to think his words through several times before he could gather the courage to ask quietly, "Now that your wife has children of her own, will I go back to my mother?" His voice was soft and low and musical, and it too was somehow disturbing. He knew that his father had been waiting for him to ask that.

"Do you want to go?" his father asked in return, leaning forward a little in his chair so that he might see his son's face more clearly.

The boy shrugged slightly. He was thinking: No, I am too much like you now; she will not want me back.

"When you first came here the decision was made by your mother and me. But you were not more than a child then; now you are old enough to decide for yourself."

His son asked carefully, "What do you want?"

"I would like you to stay," his father answered.

"So you can watch me?"

He did not mean to say that aloud. He hugged his knees and felt himself to be ugly and sinister, with his pale hair and barbed questions.

"No, little one," his father said patiently. "I don't need to watch you. And I do not care for you any less now that I have two more children."

"Who are legitimate." The child finished the sentence for him with the word that his father would not use, and hearing himself speak so made him feel still more unnatural.

"They are very small, even for twins," his father said. "The boy, the second one, may not live. If he dies you remain my only son, and you are the eldest whatever happens. You are of less importance in name alone. In trust and wisdom you can be as far superior to anyone as you dare make yourself."

The child said nothing. His father's words were calm, unaccusing and unquestioning, but he did not know how to answer them. He wished he did not have to make his father apologize for the children the man had wanted for so long. The air from the open window smelled cool and wet, and occasional stars glimmered through high, windswept clouds; the boy felt too hot, and would have liked to lean out the window into the soft spring night. But his thoughts burned through his head, flashes of lightning in the dark, and if he moved he might strike something. He held quiet. "My father, I don't want your children to die," he said, not certain he meant this, but certain his father wanted to hear him say it. "You need not excuse them to me. They had more right to be born than I had, anyway."

"All who are born have a right to be," said his father. "But I am sorry for your sake. We all told you she would never have any children. Even she thought she could not."

"And now she has two," said the boy, and thought, I wonder what she feels? He had grown to like his father's wife, stubborn and practical and quick to laugh; she spoke openly and directly, meant what she said and did not mean more than she said—so different from his own mother, who frightened all who knew her with her subtleties and mysteries.

His father spoke his name gently and said, "You must not be angry with her."

"I'm not," the child said, and added, but not aloud: She is not the one who threatens me, it is the second twin, the little boy who might not be strong enough to survive. But my father, you are as much to be blamed for his existence as she is.

He felt bruised and sore. He did not want to be in his father's house, belonging in no way except as a member of his father's family, and not really belonging there, either. Through the storm in his head he thought suddenly, I am tired.

His father spoke again. "My child, it will be a long time

before those two small ones will be a threat to you. They cannot walk, they cannot talk, they cannot think."

"Not yet," the child answered.

His father suddenly left his chair and laid heavy, gentle hands on his son's shoulders, forcing him to look toward the light. "When you are older I will make certain that you have the chance and challenge to prove yourself," he told his child. "Eight years, ten years—wait that long. Then you can do as you like, choose to serve me, travel, return to your mother in the Northern Islands. Or having done all that, you can come back. You can always come back. Only wait. By that time you will be adult, confident and competent, and the twins will still be children. You won't need to envy them, and I do not ask you to love them. Only I ask you to wait till they are grown before you decide to hate them."

The child stared at him with a still, emotionless face. Behind his blank eyes and white lashes he thought numbly, That is true—they are too small to envy or fear. He had never felt strongly enough about anything to hate it or love it.

But when he thought of the little boy, his father's youngest and most important child, some strange emotion burned through him, unrecognizable, alien. He did not know if it was hate or love or both, or something utterly different from either. It was true that the boy was barely three weeks old and smaller than any human being he had ever seen; but set in that small face were eyes so dark and radiant that they frightened him. He felt he had never seen anything more beautiful than the eyes of his small half brother, but he could not tell whether that beauty was something repulsive or attractive, hideous or wonderful.

Thinking about this, he was startled by a fleet but brightly vivid vision of how one of his fingers had been suddenly grasped in his little brother's unthinkably small ones, blindly trusting and certain. He looked up at his father and said in a low voice, "I will try to love them. You saw me take your son's hand."

"Be accurate, my young marksman," his father said. "He took yours."

1
The Marksman

When I left the Islands I had a vague image of myself fleeing from you with the speed and surety of a hart, straight to my father's estate at Camlan. The morning I left I was certain, Godmother, certain beyond anything you could have suggested to make me doubt it, that I could return to Camlan as though returning home: though it was fourteen years since the twins were born, six since I left Camlan and two since I came to you. When my father asked me to go to Brittany six years ago he had expected me back in a matter of months, and after that when I was traveling in Africa and Byzantium his letters always anticipated my return. He was not happy that I chose to remain with you over those next two summers—you, his sister; you, his enemy, treacherous and faulted as the ceiling of a mine shaft.

The morning I left you I was so desperate to be away, and free, that the very direction of the wind seemed a portent to guide me. The first fisherman I spoke to was leaving that day for the mainland, and I already carried with me all I intended to take: my hunting knife, the three bows I had crafted that summer, and a satchel containing the precious and delicate physician's instruments I had bought the year before from the Eastern sea merchants. Except these, all the possessions that I cared for I had either left in Camlan six years ago or had sent there directly as I acquired them. There was nothing to hold me to the Islands, nothing except love or fear of you. And I would not submit to either of these.

The journey's start, after the long summer of pain and illness, seemed so clean and true and swift that it did not seem possible I might be rash to travel so late in the year. The wind was perfect; we sped past the barren cliffs of Hoy, and the day was clear enough that we could see Cape Wrath looming in the distance. I have never made such a rapid journey to the mainland. I felt I had some god's own special benediction: such luck: away so quickly and secretly. Once on the soil of the mainland it occurred to me that my legs were still not very strong, that I had hundreds of miles of empty moorland to cross, and that winter was coming on. But I would not go back.

That was in October. It was well past New Year's when I arrived in Deva, the city and port closest to Camlan. There was a heavy snowfall that same day. I had not encountered snow even when I was crossing the Caledonian highlands, but now that it was steadily cold there came snow with a vengeance. I stayed in Deva several days, just to watch the harbor freeze over completely, locking its ships into my father's city: Artos the high king's city. Deva is beautiful, full of Roman ghosts. The harbor is smaller than it once was, because the river is silting up. But the streets are paved, and there is a ruined theater that they use as a marketplace. There is even a bathhouse where they still use the old hypocaust for heat. Artos probably had a hand in the last; Gofan, the master smith at Camlan, calls him "our engineer king." While I was in Deva, Artos himself arrived to inspect the harbor and make sure the old city walls were able to endure the ice. It was the first I had seen my father in six years. After the months of trudging through a wilderness of black peat mud and chill rain, alone, the pure dry cold and my father's heavy hand on my shoulder seemed more intoxicating than wine, the snowbound streets more holy than the clustering wind-scoured cells of Iona.

It is about sixty miles from Deva to Camlan, and Artos sent me on ahead of him. I went as his emissary and as his son; I went because he could not in good conscience send anyone else into that weather, and because I wanted to go. He planned a route for me, making certain I would have food and a bed each night, so the last few days of my long journey were made in relative comfort. And the countryside was achingly familiar. After Caledonia's bleak mountains even the high moors to the east seemed gentled by the snow, not shadowing but cradling the Mercian plain—beautiful. The country around Camlan is all field and forest, riddled with old Roman salt and lead mines, except in the village just two or three miles west of Camlan, where there are copper mines that Artos has set working again. The mines and the village existed long before the high king. When he rebuilt the Roman villa nearby and made it his home, the local people named the new estate Camlan, the champion's village. The original cluster of farms and householdings they now speak of simply as the village of the "elder field." The jutting cliff and scarp where the copper mines are they call the Edge over Elder Field, and it dominates the horizon even more than the distant high peaks. Camlan nestles securely between the Edge and the peaks, protected from all but the worst of weather; the forest is usually abundant with deer, the fields bountiful. It was all snow-blanketed when I arrived, uniform in whiteness.

They had had a hard summer, even as we did in the Northern Islands, in the Orcades. Everyone I met on the way seemed thin and worn: grim, haggard, hungry. They were cold, too; their winters are usually milder. It was dusk when I finally came to Elder Field, and I might have stopped for the night with Gofan at the smithy; but by now the road was so familiar that I could have walked it with my eyes shut, and I was overcome with a childish wave of homesickness for Camlan. I could not possibly wait until morning to walk the last few miles. I shared the evening meal with Gofan and Marcus, his new apprentice, and they lent me a lantern to guide me through the dark to the high king's estate.

The old Roman villa at Camlan was drab; it was cold and decaying. The echoes of its former splendor only exaggerated its cheerlessness. The tiled floor still held between its cracks the dust and pollen that had settled there during the dry summer; mildewed grain littered the corners of the central atrium, which had been used as an emergency storeroom during the haphazard harvest that was gathered in the threatening shadow of a sudden storm. Part of the hypocaust had collapsed, and someone had tried to block off the drafty hole in the atrium floor with disused masonry and rubble left over from the villa's original restoration. The old leaded glass windows, so perfect and unusual, had not been cleaned for many months. Even the braziers gave little heat. The Great Hall was warmer, with its roaring fire and close company, but after months of solitary silence and open space I found it crowded and airless almost beyond my endurance. I felt at home in the villa, ruined as it was; I knew those corridors, where each lamp bracket fits, the artist's little flaws in the tiled border of the atrium mosaic, the staring glass eyes of the Christian portraits there.

No real welcome awaited me. Of course, they did not expect me, and those of the household who were still awake were preoccupied with some present crisis. It did not seem the right moment to inquire if I could still use my old room. When my father's queen hurriedly received me I told her I would stay in the Great Hall where most of the household slept. Ginevra agreed, apologetically; they had been using my room for storage, and it would have to be cleared out before I could use it. "You'll be more comfortable in the Hall," she added. "It's warmer there. Artos is the only one who knows how the hypocaust works; we can't mend it till he returns. And"—she paused; and I could see her setting her jaw so that she would not falter—"and I think Lleu is dying. He has been ill all winter, and today he is scarcely able to breathe. Otherwise we should have given you more of a welcome, Medraut."

Lleu, the Bright One: the high king's youngest child, his heir, and my half brother. I had forgotten how sickly he was. His sister Goewin had always been healthy, and fiercely protective of her small twin brother. They were eight when I left. Lleu's letters had stopped more than three years ago, before I came to the Orcades. He would be almost fifteen

11

now, almost adult. Still so frail, racked by asthma, torn through and through by even the slightest chill wind or damp day? And Artos counted on him to be the next high king.

"Is Aquila still your physician?" I asked.

"Yes. But he's hardly slept for three days," Ginevra told me, still unfaltering.

I said cautiously, "I might help him."

"We have all been helping," she answered.

"I meant as a physician," I said.

"Truly?" She was surprised, perhaps pleased. "Well, you had to learn something in six years away from us! You do seem wiser than you did. You look the same, but there is more to your silence than there used to be."

Ginevra has the smooth, open face of a child, and she is too short and stocky to be beautiful. But she is skilled as a mapmaker, speaks three different British dialects, and knows most of the villagers by name; she manages the household with undisputed authority. Her quick appraisal made me suddenly and unexpectedly shy, though it was for a moment only. She could not have noticed. I do not color, or blanch, when I am ill at ease. I glanced down briefly at the cracked, tiled floor beneath our feet, and asked if I might see Lleu.

The corridors were dark, for Ginevra could not afford to keep lamps burning in the halls. Since Lleu had been ill he was sleeping in the antechamber to his mother's rooms, the only rooms in the house that were being steadily heated. He seemed to be asleep, or senseless, when we came in, struggling for breath with eyes clenched tightly shut; but when I sat on the cot next to him and spoke his name he tried to answer, though he could do no more than gasp and choke, lying wretchedly trapped in his ridiculous frail body. Even so I was momentarily astonished by his beauty. It struck at me as it had when I first saw him, when he was an infant. I think it is the single characteristic in him that I have always envied, will always envy. He is graceful and slightly built, like an acrobat or a cat, with black hair and brilliant dark eyes; but the eyes were closed now, the fair skin dry and fiercely hot to touch, and he did not know me.

He did not even know his mother. She tried to comfort him while I felt his forehead, gauging his fever; but when my hands moved to his throat, testing the swollen glands there, he fought me, wildly trying to tear my hands away. "You want to strangle me," he managed to whisper, coughing and struggling. I stared at Ginevra, perplexed.

"Go gently, Medraut," she cautioned wearily. "He is afraid of everything."

I bent down and said firmly, close to his ear, "Little idiot. I'm trying to help you." I brushed his own hands aside, trivial, and lifted him till he sat upright coughing and sobbing against my shoulder. With one hand I rubbed his back firmly and with the other stroked his damp hair; and gradually the coughing subsided, and he could breathe a little. He slumped against my side, whimpering and exhausted. "Keep him sitting," I murmured to Ginevra. "I can make him a drink to ease his cough. Where can I find water?"

"In the next room," she told me. "You may use anything—there're herbs and honey, as well."

I found all I needed; the room was a dressing chamber converted into a little clinic, and Aquila seemed to be keeping almost all his medicines and equipment there. The suddenness of what was happening worked on me like a drug. I could move and think with precision, knowing with accuracy what I could do for Lleu. I forgot the winter journey, the misery of the last months with you, my own uncertain welcome in my father's house. I had the sure certainty of my knowledge, and the healing in my hands. I went back to Lleu with the drink I had mixed, and held him while Ginevra coaxed him to swallow. Still he fought, this time refusing to drink when he noticed the sharp and bitter taste beneath the honey, strangely alert for all his delirium.

"Don't send me to sleep," he begged desperately, quiet and fervent. "I want to breathe, not to sleep."

"This will ease your cough, little one," I answered. "It won't make you sleep."

"Who are you?" Lleu asked abruptly. "Stay here." He choked again, and clung to me.

"I'll call for someone to watch him," Ginevra said.

"I'll stay. I don't mind."

So she left us. I eased Lleu back down onto the pillows and sat on the floor next to the cot to wait for morning.

Sometimes Lleu slept; sometimes I helped him to drink, or held him upright until he stopped coughing, or drew the covers up again when he threw them off. A servant brought me a blanket, and late in the night, when Lleu's breathing grew less ragged, I could doze a little. But most of the night I sat and watched, until the gray dawn light came stealing from behind the cloth-covered windows, and I could hear that others in the household were rising. Then I could not bear to stay awake any longer and fell asleep just as I sat: on the floor next to the bed, leaning on the mattress with my face buried in one arm and the other flung across Lleu's waist so that I should know if he stirred.

Not long afterward someone woke me and helped me to rise, and I found myself being led through the corridors in the direction of my own chamber. I felt dazed and stupid; it was a long time since I had let myself grow so exhausted. The girl who accompanied me explained that my room had been set in order for me while I had been with Lleu, and that I must feel free to come and go as I pleased within the villa. She was dark-haired, tall and long-limbed, with a somewhat hard face whose severity was tempered by humor. She seemed familiar, and at my door I asked her name. She stared at me, then laughed. I knew her then, and smiled with her, too tired to laugh. She looks more like Artos than either Lleu or I. "Princess Goewin. You must think me very foolish."

"No, no," she said. "You're half-asleep, and I have changed since I was eight. I recognized your pale hair." She opened the door to show me in and said conversationally, "You saved Lleu's life, didn't you? I insisted they open your window, so it's my fault if it's too cold in here. I remember you almost always had the window open, and it needed airing badly." There were wooden shutters instead of glass in my window, and I used to keep them open for light, not minding the cold. It touched me that Goewin had remembered. I went to the window and leaned out: the Pennines glistened clean and bare in the distance, and closer by were black trees and stone walls limned with white. "You're not wanting to go out in it again?" Goewin asked at my shoulder, narrowing her eyes against the bright light.

This time I did laugh. "No. I'm going to sleep. If Lleu gets worse, call me."

I ministered to Lleu for most of the winter. I was not so experienced as Aquila, but my knowledge of herbs and medicines reached far beyond his: for which, in all honesty, I must thank you, Aquila, who worked with the calm authority of long years of practice, accepted me as a colleague and an assistant. No one spoke openly of my skill. Some were frightened by it; was it not madness to put the life of their young prince into the hands of the high king's illegitimate son, who might know a thousand ways to poison him? But all that winter my own life centered around Lleu.

He was barely strong enough to get out of bed, and could eat only soup and thin wine. All life else for him was only the constant struggle to breathe, or to sleep fitfully, or to stare at the coals in the brazier and listen to people passing in the tiled corridor. We made him eat and saw that he was as warm as possible, and kept him bent over steaming bowls scented with mint and mustard to try to ease his breathing. He fought and fought against his illness, as though it were a physical creature that he held at bay. For long hours I fought with him. His unconscious fear of being hurt by anyone who touched him fascinated me; as far as Lleu was concerned it was a fear without foundation, but there is no emotion I could have understood more completely. When I was so badly hurt the summer before, I used to lie in dread of falling asleep; and more than that I dreaded your visits, your touch, your long fingers testing broken bones or securing bandages. But I had reason to dread you, and Lleu had no reason to dread anyone.

I knew so well how that game of fear might be played that I had to watch myself and guard against frightening him on purpose. Why is it such a great temptation to torment someone who is helpless? Lleu hated above all to be drugged into sleep, and I never allowed him to know whether the drugs I gave him would induce sleep or not. His terror at losing consciousness was so real that often he fought determinedly against nothing, against his own mind, to stay awake. I played upon his fear; though I did nothing to hurt him, nothing that could be noticed. At night when I woke sobbing or crying out against you I would vow to myself not to frighten him again. But Lleu had a sudden, imperious way of issuing questions that sounded like orders; he would demand, "Have you ever seen your real mother?" or "Tell me how you crippled your hand," and I could not bear to let such careless cruelty go unpunished. Then I would casually remark upon an increase in his fever, or speak of dreadful cures for conditions he did not have, and watch the color drain from his thin, bewitching face.

Oh, Godmother, once he asked if I had ever had a lover. What was I supposed to answer to that?

Once he asked a question that I could at least answer honestly, even if I did not like to speak of it: Had I ever killed a man. I told him, "Seven."

And he, outraged: "You keep count?"

It is a mystery to me how he manages to strike such crushing blows unintentionally. I tried to answer with dignity. He should never know whether or not he had shaken me. "I am not so callous or careless as to have yet lost track."

Chastened, he said quickly, "I'm sorry. Do you mind telling me? I can't judge you. I've never killed anything." I could not tell if there was envy or horror in his emphasis.

"I'll tell you," I said, "and you may judge me, if you like." He watched me through eyes brilliant with accusation, sitting elegantly upright against his pillows, his thin, pale hands resting quiet in the fur of one of the slim and regal cats that I had sent him from Africa. I thought how he must see me through those dark, accusing eyes: stronger and older than he, limping and dangerous. Healer and murderer. "The king—our father sent me to Brittany six years ago to deal with a Gaulish tribe that was rising against him. There was a small skirmish before the matter was settled, and I killed two of the tribesmen." I stopped, and thought, and went on. "Two other men I killed when I was helping to defend a fishing village from Saxon pirates, in a desperate fight, no more than self-defense. Also in self-defense I killed a man who attacked me on a deserted stretch of highway. That was a peculiar, ugly incident."

"And the sixth?" Lleu prompted.

"One of the men from the fishing village." It is hard for me to speak of this. "He was very badly hurt in the attack and asked me to end his life painlessly."

And suddenly from Lleu, a flash of sympathy: "That would take more courage than the others, I think. You can't help defending yourself, but to have to plan and think about a death, even a merciful death, must be terrible."

"Yes." I said to finish, my voice level, "The seventh was an execution I was asked to perform."

Lleu's pale face leached to chalk, not because he was afraid, but because that was how he registered almost any emotion. If, blameless and superior, he had demanded how I could do such a thing, I would have left him to entertain himself for the afternoon. But he said, "Who asked you to do that?"

"The queen of the Orcades."

"Aunt Morgause? Your foster mother?" Though plainly

disapproving, he was not surprised; Artos had not taught his children to look for any gentleness in you. Lleu gazed at me quizzically, and said at last, "But Medraut, you didn't want to do it."

For one blank moment I thought he had seen that in my face. Then with less assurance he added, "Did you?" It had only been a question, not insight.

"No," I answered frankly. "It was a man I had liked and trusted. There was no doubt as to his guilt, but I did not want to be his executioner."

"Why were you, then?"

"In the end, because he requested it himself." God, how cold-blooded am I? It chills me that I can speak of such a thing in idleness, without ever betraying what I felt then. I sat still and looked at Lleu directly, daring him to question me further. He said abruptly, "Your name means 'marksman.'"

"Yes. The Deft One, the Skilled One."

Lleu suddenly grinned a little, wicked and delightful. "Are you?"

Driven by mingled pride and self-contempt, I said, "I'll show you." I went into the little dressing room next door where I found a spool of thread and a light, sharp probe made of bone; then I returned to sit on the floor next to Lleu's cot. With the thread and a slender twig of kindling from the brazier I strung a makeshift bow scarcely longer than my forearm. The probe served for an arrow. I used to do this to exercise my hand when I lay bored and aching in the long hot days of the previous summer, before I was able to walk. It had been a diversion from illness and fear: so, too, for Lleu.

"Choose a target," I said.

Lleu glanced about and suggested politely, "The green cushion on the stool."

"Even you could hit that," I said. He caught the faint mockery in my voice; indignantly folding his arms, he challenged, "The eye of the middle fox in the tapestry over the door."

It was so specific and small that I think he expected me to laugh and ask for a reasonable target; or if I did not, to come close but miss, and afterward receive his condescending praise. I was too proud to do either. I never miss.

"Go on," Lleu said, waiting.

"Watch closely," I said. "There's hardly any strength in a bow this small; the probe will probably bounce off the cloth when it strikes." Lleu's gaze flickered dubiously from the stiff and scarred fingers of my left hand to the target he had chosen: but what is my hand weighed against my name, my nature? I drew back the almost invisible bowstring, and shot; the sharp little sliver of bone struck straight through the minute black knot of embroidery, and pinned the cloth fast to the door.

"Oh, well done!" Lleu cried. He sat up straight, white and thrilled, and the startled and offended cat stalked away from him. Lleu stared hard at the door, then shivered and turned to stare at me. "I have to trust you utterly, don't I?"

What made him say that, what made him aware of that? I shrugged as if I neither minded nor understood what he meant; but I was making light of what was true.

11

Equinoctial

I dreamed of you, Godmother. When I was traveling I slept deep and sound; once back in Camlan I found myself stricken with frequent and unsettling dreams, always of you, always hateful. They were the final scars you left on me. I tried to ignore and forget them as I did the marks you left on my body; but like those, I could not always hide them. By chance, one night, when Lleu was terrifying the household with his panicked gasping, someone sent Goewin to wake me. I have no idea what I revealed to her that first night, for when I woke I could not remember the dream. Goewin would not repeat what she had heard me say, not even to me. But after that night if I was needed she came for me without being told. She would wake me carefully, rarely touching me, with a low word in my ear or a light in my eyes. Sometimes I mistook her for you, and then she would speak to me quietly and steadily until I woke and knew otherwise. There were those who thought me treacherous: what blazing fuel to that fire if Goewin had repeated the oaths and protests I made to you in my sleep. But she never told anyone else.

I tried to lock you out of my mind. I let the empty calm of the snowbound fields envelop me. I cared for Lleu or rode alone; sometimes I visited Gofan at the smithy, or read, or helped stoke the fires under the granary floor that kept the corn dry. By spring I could walk without limping, and my ruined hand did not ache so much with the cold or damp. The dreams I bore, hating them, as I bore and hated Lleu's careless arrogance.

Spring did not come gradually, with indistinct changes in the air and earth, but all at once. One morning the snow was gone. Artos came back barely a day later. The winter must have been as dreadful for him as for any of us, knowing or guessing at his child's illness and being held in Deva by cold and responsibility. All Camlan was cheered when he returned, and Ginevra held a mock banquet in his honor. We dressed in our finest clothes and brightened the dark beams of the Great Hall with garlands of holly that Goewin told me had never gone up at Christmas; the small ration of bread for the meal was twisted into individual loaves in the shapes of birds, flowers, and fish.

In the evening before the feast Artos took me into his study as he used to do, to talk with me in earnest and in private. When I was younger the hours spent there had been a privilege and an honor, and the room itself still seemed to offer me the promise of authority and fulfilled ambition. It is one of the smaller and darker chambers in the villa, but familiar and comfortable: it is Britain and Artos in essence, peculiarly his people's and his own. The dark wood cabinets are stocked with tax receipts and harvest reports from all the islands and from Brittany, and there are shelves and shelves of Ginevra's precise and careful maps. Artos and Ginevra share the drafting board and stencils, straightedges and measures; but unique to Artos himself is the clay model of the city wall at Deva, and the entire wall behind his desk is covered by a linen tapestry intricately embroidered with the floor plan of his beloved villa. With her unerring eye for distance and contour, Ginevra made it for him twenty years ago, after he had so painstakingly rebuilt the vast old house and settled the heart of his kingdom at Camlan. On countless evenings as a child I sat or stood here before my father, telling him of the exciting or trivial events of my days; and here six years ago Artos gave me the first real chance to prove myself worthy of his trust, when he sent me to Brittany to exercise a strict yet merciful disciplinary expedition in his name.

On this night we talked at length of my travels, and of the distant places I had seen and the people I had come to know. I spoke with esteem and affection of Kidane, the merchant I had stayed with when I served as an ambassador to the African kingdom of Aksum, and of his daughter Turunesh, who had become my dear friend. Artos asked me once if I would speak of the time I spent with you, but I would tell him nothing except that I had left you estranged. It was then that I advised him to send for your younger children to foster himself. I knew your lord King Lot of the Orcades would be pleased to have his sons reared at the court of their uncle the high king, and that you would be powerless to prevent them from coming. I was cold, speaking of this. Artos did not press me further concerning you: he hides dark memories enough of his own.

He spoke then of Lleu. I had not expected such confidence; it took me off-guard. I found myself shy and silent, and absurdly flattered. For he told me this:

"You must know how I love Lleu. He is my youngest child, and a joy to me; but no one has ever expected him to survive to adulthood. This winter has been the worst, and I believe he is alive now only because of you. I will admit to you freely that I was afraid my sister might poison your mind against me and my queen's children. Your devotion to Lleu these last three months has assuredly proved that fear to be unfounded. But Lleu's illness has also proved that though I may still cherish the hope that he will live to be my heir, I cannot afford to be so blinded by love for him as to count on it.

"And this is how I will shape the future of the kingship. So long as he lives, Lleu is my first legitimate son and my heir. When he becomes sixteen I will have him declared prince of Britain. He is well loved by his people, but as a child is loved, as a rare jewel is guarded, as a symbol—the Bright One, the sun lord's namesake. He is physically weak, he is soft of heart to the point where he will not even hunt, and he does not have the head for difficult judgments. He has no real talent, nothing I can see in him that will make him into any kind of warrior or administrator.

"But you are different. Medraut, I am going to train you in everything I know. I want you to be able to cope with the tax receipts and revenue reports, as well as the governing of the harvest and defense systems. You know you can never be called high king; if Lleu dies I must make Goewin my heir. Even if Lleu survives, chances are the real power will lie in your hands no matter what name I give him. And I would rather have you at his side, using your superior skill and strength and wisdom for his support, than plotting to overthrow him. I will name you regent, and you will be the backbone, the keystone to his kingship."

Through this I sat speechless with my hands clenched, quivering in delight and tension. My father's praise meant more to me than I can say. And the regency, the captaincy, the responsibility to be mine—it seemed to me then that it could not possibly matter who received the title.

"I had thought to start by giving you a shared foremanship in the copper mines at Elder Field," Artos said. "There is a foreman in one of the more difficult tunnels who is also a landholder, and he cannot devote as much time to the seam as it needs. You can relieve him and still have half your days for your own pursuits and for learning the core of whatever else I must teach you. It is only a beginning, but your life and position will be secure. I will see to that. I know that you are capable of leading men, and of holding together what I have built. Will you accept the position in the mines?"

"With all my heart!" I answered without hesitation. "Sir—oh, my father, there is nothing I would rather do."

He laughed a little at my fervor and said, "I also ask a favor: that you try to impart to Lleu something of your own wisdom. He is unfinished. He is not full grown and is not very strong, he is easily frightened and often thoughtless. He needs to be crafted and straightened, like an arrow, and set in the right direction. My marksman, see if you can make him worthy of his name."

"I will accept that challenge too," I answered.

After that, we went together to the Great Hall to celebrate with the rest of the household. It was a time of new expectancy and hope, promise of an end to hunger and sickness, an end to stillborn children and bony livestock, and to all the fight to make the previous year's poor harvest last till the next. We were glad of that spring.

The weeks that followed were full with new work and knowledge. Artos made me one of his Comrades, gracefully bringing me into his select band of warriors and counselors an entire year before his heir would become one of them. The mining too was a joy and a consolation to me. The mines at Elder Field are not large, though some of the natural tunnels go very deep; anyone looking for work can help in the less dangerous shafts and surface quarries. I had, when I was younger. Now I shared supervision of one of the deeper shafts with a man called Cado, each of us usually working only half the day. Cado was a solid man with a square face, devoted to his farm as well as to the mining; his initial uncertain deference to me soon fell away to reveal kindness and keen but gentle wit. The tunnel we worked together was dangerous and unpredictable, but that made the work worthwhile. The six men under our command were quick and clever as well as strong. We knew what we were doing, or we learned. Faulted ceilings we shored with rock and oak; newly dug passages we tested for poisonous air. I liked the even darkness, the even temperature summer or winter, the wet walls of mineral and clay glittering green and red. I liked Cado, and I liked the companionship of the other six I worked with, the respect they showed me and the responsibility I must show them.

In the evenings Artos and I played draughts, or I pored over maps with Ginevra. My small room was stacked with boxes I had sent from Byzantium and Africa, six years' worth of books, tools, clothes, ornaments, and gifts that I had not seen since I acquired them. I unpacked these things slowly; sometimes Lleu and Goewin helped or watched, fascinated by the mysterious assortment of foreign goods. The twins coaxed me to read to them, or to tell them stories of the distant lands I had seen. I drew comfort from my small chamber and the simple things that surrounded me: the African cats that wandered in and out, the mosaic floor with its three dancing dolphins, the view of the high peaks in the distance, the infant bats in the little box hung outside the window. Once, near evening, Goewin found me outside the house reaching with cupped hands toward the bat box, and she inquired what I held. I stood a moment considering whether she would be frightened or delighted if I showed her, then opened my hands a little to reveal one of the baby bats, a tiny silver thing. "They eat insects," I explained. "Would you like to hold it?"

"Could I?" Goewin said, as though she hardly dared touch something so exotic and fragile. "Will it let me?"

"I think so," I said, giving the warm, exquisite creature into her hands. "They are learning to trust me."

In April the twins were fifteen. In one more year Artos intended to declare Lleu as prince of Britain, the heir to his kingdom. Lleu, the prince of Britain: one could scarcely believe it to look at him, fragile and pale as he was. I worked to make him stronger. I saw that he had plenty to eat, sharing my own food with him when I thought he did not have enough. There was no hunting to be done at this time of year, but the horses must be exercised; we went on long, easy rides through the raw and muddy countryside. Often Goewin came with us. To Lleu it must have been like a release from prison, to be out of the crowded and dark confines of the Great Hall, or the dreary chill of the villa. I was fiercely glad of the joy and strength he took from the weak, watery sunlight and the smell of damp earth, the cold daffodils and quickening hazel.

Lleu and Goewin also went out on their own, exploring field and forest and the red sandstone contours of the Edge over Elder Field. Goewin has always been a skilled rider and was trying to teach Lleu stunts and jumps; but Lleu did not even share her strength then, let alone her ability. I often came upon them practicing and would watch them racing madly through the unplowed fields, and sometimes I joined them uninvited. I never spoke a single word of disapproval. But I did not like to see Lleu vaulting walls and streams. They both sensed this and were vaguely resentful when I was with them, subdued and ill at ease. I swore to be damned before I let Lleu resent me: no one commanded my compassion. I was neither nurse nor guardian, and he could ride where and how he liked. So when the two began to slip out after dark to ride by moonlight, I told no one and did not try to stop them. When Lleu disastrously ended these escapades by breaking his arm I did not blame myself.

But they came to me for help that night, after all, rather than anyone else. I answered the tentative tapping on my door to find Goewin, for once as pale as her brother, supporting a fainting and battered Lleu. No questions, then; without thinking I caught Lleu in my arms and carried him to my bed as though he were a child of five, not fifteen. As I cut away the shredded remnants of his jacket and shirt I could not help but murmur, "Good God, Princess; what have you done to him? After I spent most of the winter trying to keep him alive, you half kill him in one night."

Goewin stood in the doorway and watched miserably. "We went riding," she said. "I said we should gallop, and I got ahead of him—we had to leap a stream, and he was going too fast to stop. It was dark; he missed the jump and was thrown. I—I couldn't stop it happening—" Her voice shook. It had been her fault, and she knew it. She knew the limits of Lleu's skill better than anyone.

"Don't cry, little Princess," I said. "He's not dying."

That made her angry. "Little Princess" stung her. She stood in the doorway a moment gazing at me wrathfully, then choked out, "I'll get you some water." She left the room in a quiet storm, black hair tossing, her hands shut in tight fists.

I lit a lantern. The left sleeve of Lleu's jacket had been almost sheared off, and I guessed he must have been hurled sideways, landing on the arm and then sliding. One bone was broken cleanly and decisively, beneath skin that was brush-burned raw from shoulder to elbow. "Where else did you hit?" I asked.

Lleu spoke through his teeth. "All that side—I don't know."

"Your head?"

"No." He lay taut and still, with his eyes closed and his fists clenched. Except for the arm I could see no severe hurt on him, only bruises and scrapes. Goewin came back and without a word set a jug of water by me on the floor, and turned to stir the coals in the brazier until she had coaxed a small fire into flame. After that she perched on the edge of the cot next to Lleu's head, out of my way. She watched as I examined Lleu's slender body, more mindful than Lleu himself of my long fingers testing the dark bruises. It would have been so easy to hurt him. But I could not forget my own helpless apprehension the summer before, as I lay under your hands, defenseless as Lleu and more desperately wounded.

"Nothing is broken but the arm," I said at length. "Will you help me, Goewin?"

She did help me. She obeyed me, followed my directions and worked with me, but she would not look at my face or speak to me until I reached to the floor for the water jug, and the loose robe I wore slipped down my back. Then with smooth fingers Goewin traced the long, ragged scars across my shoulder blade, pale claw marks; there was such gentleness and pity in her touch. "What made these?" she whispered.

My body is seamed with scars. How is it she saw only those? I murmured, "What made any of them?" and jerked the sleeve back up across my shoulder, wishing that she had neither touched me nor spoken. I bent to clean the abrasions across Lleu's arm and knew without looking at her that Goewin still stared at me.

"What," she said in an unsteady voice, "have you been doing these past six years that you have gained so many hurts and so much wisdom?"

Lleu lay listening, waiting tense beneath my hand for me to hurt and heal him. Anything I said could frighten him. "I cannot tell you now," I answered Goewin without hesitation. My stiff fingers were steady against Lleu's broken arm, and I was suddenly grateful for his trust and fear.

Together Goewin and I splinted and bandaged Lleu's

arm, and washed and anointed the scrapes. There was little more we could do for him. "Have you put away your horses?" I asked. Goewin nodded. "Go to bed, then," I said. "Lleu can stay here tonight."

"But where will you—," Goewin began.

"I've blankets enough for both of us. There's no sense in moving him now."

She saw that there was not, but would not be dismissed so abruptly. "I'll stay till you're ready," she said, and bent over and kissed her twin. "I'm sorry," she whispered in his ear, not meaning me to hear. "Oh, Lleu, I am so sorry—"

"It wasn't your fault," Lleu whispered back. "Thank you."

Goewin stayed sitting next to Lleu, and I began to put things away and to spread blankets on the floor for myself. It occurred to me that Lleu's arm would keep him awake, and I mixed poppy and wine for him. I brought it to the bedside, lifted his head and shoulders gently, and held the bowl to his lips. "Drink."

"What is it?"

"To lessen the pain."

Lleu drank gratefully, and I lowered him again. But I stayed next to him, watching. "It wasn't Goewin's fault," Lleu said. "I suggested we go out at night."

It was a silver-washed night of a waxing moon; I could not blame them for wanting to be out in it. "You have received just punishment for so foolhardy a suggestion," I said. "Your sister ought to be punished for encouraging it."

"I probably will be, sir," Goewin said fiercely.

Lleu, lying still with closed eyes, said suddenly, "Medraut."

"Little one?"

31

"That drink," Lleu said. "Is it sending me to sleep?"

I watched him without feeling anything, as though I were watching from a distance. "Yes."

"You know he hates to be made to sleep," Goewin said angrily. "You do it on purpose."

"It will be easier for him," I said, now feeling amused at their indignation.

"I hate it," Lleu said, and struggled to sit up.

Lleu enraged: the Bright One. Helpless and splendid. "Lie still, little one; lie still." Goewin's eyes on me were stony. "Don't fight."

But Lleu fought. I always underestimate the strength of his will. "You must promise me you'll not do it again," he said, struggling to stay awake and furious that he could not. "I'd rather be in pain."

"I won't do it without good cause." Am I that cruel? "I don't do it now without good cause. You'll shock your parents well enough tomorrow without having spent a night without sleep."

"Sir, you didn't even ask him!" Goewin said.

Allied against me.

"Medraut, listen to me," Lleu said. His eyes were closed and he spoke slowly and very quietly. "I command you—*I command you* not to use on me in the future, no matter how ill or hurt I am, anything that might make me sleep, without my consent. Swear."

I sat with my head bent. I must seem hard and proud of body and spirit, aloof and most at ease in my cold, austere surroundings; but I woke without complaint or question in the middle of the night to assist and care for them, the children who had usurped my place in my father's heart and hearth. "I promise," I said, hesitating a little, "not to send you to sleep at any time you might be ill or hurt, from now on." Lleu's rigid body had relaxed. "Did you understand that?" I asked. I turned to Goewin, inquiring. Lleu murmured something brief and inaudible. "Even if you didn't understand," I said in quiet, "that is a promise I will keep." I bent over and kissed Lleu as easily and honestly as Goewin had, then stood and held out a hand to help her rise. At the door she turned and looked at me straight.

"Well," she said carefully, "it is behind you now." She did not mean the promise I had just made. Her words touched me with the cool surety of her fingertips. She had come to me for help; she trusted me even without fear, although she knew how you haunted me. "Thank you, Medraut," she said.

33

111
Edges

The secret of my birth tore at me. It seemed strange that even when he spoke to me alone, Artos always referred to you as my aunt or my foster mother. But I asked him if I might tell the twins the truth. It seemed important that they know, especially Lleu, so that their acceptance of who and what I was could be completely unclouded. Vain of me, selfish and probably irrelevant; but Lleu must know the real reason I could not be made my father's heir, the reason that went deeper than mere bastardy. Artos agreed. So I told them; I told them that you are my real mother, and that your brother Artos is my father.

On hearing this the Bright One immediately informed me, "But that's incest," and I could not help answering coldly, "So it is."

When you took him, Artos had not yet been told who his parents were and could not have guessed that you were his sister. I impressed upon Lleu and Goewin their father's blamelessness, and avoided any judgment of you and your part. Nor did I tell them what Artos suspected afterward, and what you told me yourself, that you had wittingly made love to him so you might use any child you bore to him as a weapon against him. That knowledge in itself is terrible enough for me to live with, but the incest . . . I wish Lleu had been able to say something else when I first told him. That single sordid night of my father's life dwindles to insignificance in the black light of my own shame.

So, they knew now, and that secret was shared. Finally I could shut away the thought of you, just as I hid the dragon bracelets from Cathay that I could neither bring myself to wear nor to give away. And I no longer dreamed of you.

It was a gentle summer, and when I was not at work I was often with Lleu and Goewin. Inwardly I longed for their companionship, and the two sometimes allowed me within their circle. Not completely, and not always. But enough. We visited the smithy; we flew my Oriental kites of red and gold paper from the top of the Edge. We rode together, and spent long hours exploring the surrounding country. And twice I took Lleu and Goewin into the copper mines. The first time was by day, with Artos. We stood in the entrance of the cavern that leads to the main workings, and Cadarn the chief foreman explained to the twins how the copper ore is removed and how the shaft entrances are reinforced with stone lintels. But I am not sure they saw anything beyond an impression of the intriguing black, hollow place before them, shot through with darts of flame and glinting water, and echoing with the voices of men and the sound of metal against rock. The second time I took them was by night.

During the long spring mornings Artos was rebuilding the floor and heating system of the villa; he was painstakingly prying up sections of tile and replacing the crumbling hollow clay bricks that lay beneath the atrium. The exposed catacomb of the hypocaust had the look of a miniature crypt, ancient and airless, so old and grim that while the floor was uncovered Lleu would not walk through the atrium by himself after dark. One night I challenged him: "Would you see real darkness?"

Goewin, fearless, said, "Show us." So that night I took them back to the mines. We made our way quietly through the young fields to the forest and the Edge; Lleu's broken arm kept us from being able to climb, so we took the safest and most open paths. But beneath the Edge there is only the earth itself, and there the concept of safety becomes brittle and trivial. We stood in the first cavern, quiet now, and Lleu's face was waxen in the light of his taper.

"Look up," I said.

The first cave is wide, long, and low-ceilinged. The rock roof is rippled and smooth, like the muscles in a horse's back. "It's like the sand at the coast," Goewin said. "It's beautiful."

Lleu said, "We mustn't go in very far."

"No," I answered. I did not laugh.

I marked the walls with charcoal when we came to turnings. Lleu and Goewin had only seen these tunnels full of the movement of men pulling carts and cutting stone. The carts stood at rest now, and the stone lay in heavy piles or jutted strangely and unnaturally from the walls where it had been hewn. The caves are no darker by night than by day; our candle flames cut the darkness softly, like a hand parting hair, not a chisel shaping rock. We kept to wide, straight, level

36

passages, for the tunnels and caverns connect and cross, run parallel and above and below one another. It is a quiet, secret place. At night it seems to return to its former silence, the silence of the inside of the earth, ignoring the little pickings of the miners during the quick days.

"This is all yours, Lleu," Goewin said suddenly. "When you're high king, this will be part of your kingdom too."

"Dare anyone say he owns this?" Lleu said.

"Surely not one who is afraid of the dark," I answered quietly.

He hated that. He hated it, and never argued: we stood two hundred feet below the surface of the earth, and only I knew the way out. Even Goewin said nothing in his defense. The prince of Britain, and afraid to walk through his own house at night! Well, he was not prince of Britain yet.

Perhaps I managed to shame him with my derision, and now he learned to disguise his fear. After that night, as his father replaced the atrium floor, Lleu followed behind, filling in and matching the broken stretches of mosaic with chips of glass and malachite and azurite. After he had glimpsed the abyss, the low dusty hollow place beneath the villa no longer frightened him. But I had not finished with this lesson in darkness.

One afternoon in deep July I rode north and east with Lleu and Goewin, straight across the green country toward the high moors on the horizon, through the forested park where the high king's deer and boar grew fat, across one of the old, straight Roman roads paved with heavy flagstones. Beyond that we followed a little river between steep wooded hills, and left behind us the poppy-lit fields. The way grew steeper; behind and below us the oak and birch leaves shone green in the sun, and the river snaked away in runnels of diamond light. Above, the high, flat peak that one can just glimpse from the top of the Edge was shrouded in cloud and mist. I know the moors well enough, but Lleu and Goewin had never been here before.

"Shall I take your reins?" I asked Lleu as the steep land beneath the horses' hooves grew stony and riddled with tufts of bracken. The trees about us thinned and dropped away.

"I can manage," Lleu said fiercely. His riding had improved, but because of his broken arm the reins still gave him trouble. Caius, the high king's steward, was teaching Lleu to ride in the Roman fashion so that he might control the horse more with his knees than his hands.

"The ground will get rougher," I explained in apology. "Well, be careful."

We left the trees behind. The ground cover was all heather and gorse, brilliant violet and gold. The air was still; foamy, scattered clouds swung low in the sky, sometimes blocking the sun, sometimes not. The lowest clouds tore on the summit of the hill we were climbing, making a shredded curtain of mist beyond which nothing was visible. "Where are we going?" Goewin asked.

"This is the highest of the peaks you can see on the horizon from Camlan," I said. "Have you never climbed any of them?" I knew they had not. Looking straight ahead of me toward the crest of the peak, riding serenely a little forward of my young sister and brother, I said, "Well, you have already seen the dark below. This is perhaps the abyss inverted."

Goewin, with a brief snort of indignation, pulled forward till she rode abreast of me, and said in a cold, inquisitive voice, "Sir? 'The abyss inverted'? I don't understand."

"The dark above. Not literal darkness, as in the mines, but a place of mystery all the same. When we ride into the mist, look about you."

We entered the fog. Beads of water hung like amethysts on the heather. Behind us where the ground fell away the cloud came down like a screen, hiding the countryside below. Only the river could be seen, a shining streak of light slashing through the white wall of fog at an incongruous angle. The mist hid the land between ourselves and the river, and the faraway line of water looked as though it were suspended in midair.

"Why does it glitter?" Lleu asked.

"The sun is shining down there," Goewin told him. "It's only we who are in cloud."

We rode on. The heather gave way to bare peat now, and the country became strange. Even as little as ten miles to the south the moors are gentler than these reaches of bog. "We could get very lost," Lleu said.

"We could," I said. "The fog could be many times as thick. If it were we would stay in one place till it cleared. As it is, we keep the river in sight." Behind us we could still see the river, a wire of pure silver suspended in the white, empty air.

Within our circle of mist the peat was black, the air gray. Sudden gullies of water gushed here and there over dark slides of earth. We no longer climbed; the peak flattens near the summit, and we rode on almost level ground along the edge of the top of the hill. Measures of bog stretched away from us toward the highest point, hidden by cloud; vast outcroppings of rock loomed out of the fog, looking at first like huts or groups of people or withered trees, then becoming stones again as we passed by. The horses stepped cautiously between low clots of turf that rose above the mud and were rooted together by clumps of short, coarse grass. Three gray birds flew off into the mist in a flurry of clapping and cracking wings, and twice we heard the loud, strident crying of some disturbed moor bird. That was all we encountered of other living beings. At last we came to a wide, flat, shallow stream with unexpectedly white sandy banks like the mouth of a river; on the near bank stood a cairn of piled loose rock. We dismounted and added a few pebbles to the cairn, drank from the stream, and ate a luncheon of honey, bread, cheese, and eggs. We talked while we ate, for when we were silent we were too much aware of how alone we were, and how lost we could be.

"On a clear day it might be lovely up here," Goewin said.

"Then why should Medraut think it an evil place?" Lleu muttered.

"No one spoke of evil," I said lightly. "Only of mystery, and darkness."

"Like the mines," Lleu said slowly, understanding. "This is real, but it doesn't threaten you. You don't have to come here. Father holds back the real evil—the pirates and invaders from the sea, the painted people from the north— treats with them and keeps them at ease."

"It's no easy thing to treat with the Sea Wolves," I said.

Goewin added thoughtfully, "You have to—you have to be able to imagine what they are thinking. It's not like feeding hounds and having them be loyal to you. Hounds don't plan; they don't think."

"But the Saxons think wrong," Lleu said.

"Only according to you!" Goewin laughed. "The raiders

from the warships may be evil, but not all Saxons are evil, certainly not those who have settled here in peace. You can't just dismiss them all. And not all your own folk are good, either. What will you do if a treaty is broken? What will you do if you find treachery within?"

Lleu laughed also. "When I find treachery within I'll call on you, suspicious one. I can continue Father's defense."

"But it isn't just a matter of defense!" Goewin pressed. "You have to be able to change, to know whether to attack or to organize new treaties yourself, even if you're not sure they'll work—you have to stand your ground but be fair to your enemy at the same time. That's what Father really does. You have to learn to take risks."

In fierce rapture, I watched their faces as the twins worked their way through the last argument. "Have you thought long on the government of a kingdom, Goewin?" I asked. Oh, she of all of us has always and only been the true child of the high king: Artos the Dragon and Artos the Bear, forbidding and forgiving, who holds a few tottering and assaulted peoples together as a single, peaceful kingdom.

We turned back. We broke into sunlight again, and began the journey home across that broad, bright country.

I V
The Bright One

In the midst of that mild summer Lleu learned to use a
sword. Bedwyr, whom Artos calls most trusted of advisers
and best of friends, took over Lleu's training in swordsmanship even before I had taken the splints from Lleu's arm.
Bedwyr had lost his left hand in one of the high king's early
battles, but despite this remained the most accomplished
swordsman I had ever known. When Lleu's broken arm kept
him from his usual swordplay Bedwyr suddenly noticed him,
and appointed himself Lleu's tutor. At first he and Lleu did
not practice with weapons; to watch them you would think
that Lleu was learning some kind of tight, dangerous dance.
The two of them spent their afternoons dodging and circling
each other. When Lleu's arm was sound enough to bear some
occasional battering, Bedwyr bound it to Lleu's side to keep it
steady and they began using wooden swords.

Lleu's fledgling talent was so startling that at first they

did not dare to speak of it. Bedwyr, whose blunt and heavy countenance rarely breaks out of its frown, is not one to be lavish with praise; but I heard him once growl at Artos, "I don't know what made you think Caius can teach your son to use a sword. Lleu can't hack things down by sheer force, he's too light. But you watch. He's a rare one. In a year he'll be able to disarm you." In time Lleu's arm was whole again; together he and Bedwyr made it almost as strong and capable as the right, until Lleu could manage a sword with either hand. He improved rapidly as a young deer might grow, and he began to develop a skill that we could all see was nearly as deadly as his master's. Lleu danced. He was too quick to catch, and too agile to hold. I do not think it was more to him then than a dance, a game; the swords he used were only of wood, or dull. But his excitement in the swordplay kindled to precision, speed, a sapling strength in his arms and back. I had thought him the slight one, the fragile one: his skill was frightening.

I thought I was content. At long last I could hunt again; I had not brought down anything larger than a rabbit in over a year, and now we hunted wolf, deer, and boar for their hides and the winter's meat. The challenge and chase were exhilarating. Parties of us spent days at a time on foot with spears in the vast forest south of Camlan, and then we would bring back four or five large kills at once. But best I liked to ride out alone, or in small parties of two and three, and to hunt with the bow.

The harvest was not bountiful, but sufficient. That in itself was reason to celebrate, and we set beacons flaming across the land in thanksgiving. There were bonfires on the Edge over Elder Field to the west and on Shining Ridge to the east, and we danced between these at Camlan, the heart of all the lights. Lleu had been absorbed for weeks with a group of traveling jugglers and tumblers who had assisted in the reaping and storing of grain. He had never forgotten the few somersaults and handsprings taught him as a child; he was now graceful and supple as he had been then, but stronger. The performers were enamored of him, and on the harvest night they masked him in copper and amber as his namesake, Lleu Llaw Gyffes, the Lord of the Sun. They made him tumble as they had taught him, tossed him and caught him, and called him "prince of acrobats" and "prince of dancers."

You need not think of me standing apart from the revelers and watching sullenly just beyond the circle of firelight, the slow cancer in the beating heart. I danced and drank with the rest of them. Late in the evening, when the dancing was over and we sat at our ease around the dying bonfires, I set off the colored flares I had from Cathay, and fire snappers that consume themselves with loud bursts of flame. I told the courageous story of Turunesh, the African woman who gave them to me, how she and her father Kidane had left Aksum and traveled halfway across the world to find such things. Those who were still awake listened with wonder and pleasure, so that I felt myself to be one of all, trusted, accepted, and admired among the high king's companions.

Of the autumn and the following winter I remember little, only certain moments that are bright rimmed in my mind's eye with the clarity of lightning. All were blows to the tumultuous feelings for Lleu that I fought to master, and the incidents formed a kind of pattern leading to the moment when Artos officially named his son prince of Britain. The earliest was after a day of hunting, when Lleu told me in a voice despising and superior, "You're certainly bloodthirsty."

Lleu did not hunt. That is, he rode with us, and helped to dress the meat, but his shots always went wide. At first I had thought he was simply a poor marksman, and I wondered that he had not been better trained. But it was difficult to believe that such a matchless swordsman could be so careless of precision with a bow in his hand. Lleu chose with purpose to miss his mark; he could kill, but would not. I answered, "Are you so noble, to let others kill your winter's meat for you?"

To which Goewin added, "I like hunting—am I bloodthirsty too?"

"Don't be silly," Lleu said. "You aren't so intent on the destruction of life as Medraut is."

I at least can heal as well as kill.

Bloodthirst was not all that Goewin and I had in common. One autumn afternoon, while she was roaming the colonnaded porch that opens off the atrium, she came upon me sitting on the wide stone steps that lead down to the Queen's Garden. I was fitting feathers to arrows, and Goewin sat next to me to watch. It is a task I enjoy, calling for deft hands, and perfect judgment and balance. Goewin sat companionably for a few minutes without speaking or interrupting me; then suddenly she asked, "How did you hurt your hand?"

I looked at the hills in the distance for a moment, then glanced at her briefly. "Stag hunting on foot," I said. I will not lie. "I was nearly killed. The bones of my fingers were . . . set badly, and had to be broken and set over again."

She answered as coolly as I had spoken to her. "They don't bother you."

"No longer."

"Your arrows are beautiful," Goewin stated simply. I really did look at her then, and smiled a little in honest appreciation.

"I wasn't changing the subject," she added.

"I know," I said. "But the hand looks worse than it is. It doesn't hinder me." I bent to my work and added in jest, "Though my arrows would be beautiful in any case."

Goewin laughed. "You sound like Lleu."

"How?"

"Sure of yourself. Lleu is so sure of himself! How do you bear his insults and commands with such grace? Sometimes he makes me want to strike him."

"Well . . . Diana and Apollo may quarrel," I said.

"Who are they?" Goewin asked, interested.

I smiled. "The old Roman goddess and god of the moon and sun. They're twins, like you. There is a story where they argue over which of them is the better archer; there is not much doubt in your case."

"Who will notice Lleu's poor aim," Goewin said, "now that he can defend himself against Britain's greatest swordsman?"

"You're not jealous?" I asked.

Goewin scooped a handful of brown, dry leaves from the flagstones and spread them over her skirt. It was a gown she had worn for two years, and was too short for her. In spite of the chill she was barefoot. But no one ever scolded her for that as they did Lleu; suddenly I saw her a little neglected. "No," she answered me. "After all, I could never manage a sword." She scattered the leaves about her dusty feet. "Only . . ."

"Only you could manage a kingdom," I said.

In a voice so soft it was almost a whisper, Goewin said, "Yes. I think I could."

"You see, Princess," I said quietly, "you and I are not so different."

When we walked inside together Lleu was sitting on the floor of the atrium beneath one of Ginevra's pot-bound lemon trees, toying with an unfinished corner of the mosaic. The chips of colored stone glinted in the heavy afternoon sun that poured through the old glass windows. Lleu was absorbed and at ease, vaguely graceful even in the way he sat, head bent, thinking, motionless. When he noticed Goewin he leaped to his feet and whirled her in a short, wild dance across the tesserae, scattering a few unused tiles that clicked beneath their feet and shot across the floor like thrown stones skimming over ice. The twins half sat, half fell into one of the stone ledges set in the windows as seats. "What is it?" Goewin laughed.

"I've beaten Bedwyr," Lleu announced.

"You've what?" Goewin said, hardly able to take him seriously.

"Four times today I disarmed him."

Astounded, Goewin said, "*Today?* You disarmed Bedwyr *four times* today?"

Lleu's dark eyes sparkled and his face glowed. He nodded. He would never say such a thing if it were not true.

"How on earth did you manage that?" Goewin asked shakily.

"From learning all that tumbling. He didn't know where

47

I'd be—he couldn't hold me. Oh, Goewin, we were so pleased!"

"Lleu," Goewin said carefully, glancing up at me, "Bedwyr is considered the finest swordsman in the kingdom."

"I know," Lleu said softly.

"But you must be—Lleu, you can't be that good in one summer's training!"

"Ask Bedwyr," Lleu said. "Anyway, it isn't really one summer. I'd learned to use a sword before Bedwyr began to teach me. He teaches skill."

"He couldn't ever teach Caius enough skill to disarm him," Goewin said. She stared at her twin. "You must be simply brilliant. And nobody ever noticed it!"

"I've never been well enough before," Lleu said. "Oh, Goewin, I can't tell you how"—he laughed—"how remarkable I feel. Aren't I?"

Goewin tried to push him out of the window seat; but she could no longer best him in strength. She laughed instead. "Yes, you conceited creature, you are remarkable."

But I could not laugh.

Artos was not in Camlan when this happened. He was making his seasonal progress through the south of Britain, checking defenses and supplies in the small towns and cities. Lleu wrote to tell him of the occasion, and Artos wrote back exulting: "Lleu, my Bright One, you will make a king, after all—think of it, the finest swordsman in Britain at fifteen! I'll begin to train you as I've trained Medraut. . . . Stay strong, grow wise, and I'll crown you with pride in the spring."

Such love in those words, such love and joy. It was never Lleu's name that I envied.

On a November morning a few weeks later I walked with Lleu and Goewin to Elder Field to visit the smithy. It was the first day in two weeks that the sky was clear; the air was chill but not cold. The track across the surrounding fields that leads to the wooded Edge and the mines was so muddy that we almost had to wade. Men were out setting the hedges and cutting back the hazel coppices, glad for the respite from the rain. We kept close to the edge of the wood; the trees glittered with drops of water, and wet dead leaves clung to our ankles. When we arrived at the smithy, Gofan greeted us cordially, though shortly, and over the ringing din that Marcus was making indicated that we should stay out of the way. But despite the furious clatter and the heat they were producing, the two were not particularly hard at work that day. In this late autumn time of hedge laying and hunting they had set aside the constant repair and production of harness and yoke fixtures, scythe blades and plowshares that kept the smithy busy earlier in the year. Gofan was teaching his young apprentice a more intricate work, and they were making a gate or screen of wrought iron.

After a time the two men left their work quiet and came over to sit and talk with us. Sunlight streamed in across the floor from the open porch, turning to shadow now and again as the clouds moved across the sky, making the coals in the forge grow brighter for a moment. "What have you been up to in your Roman villa?" Marcus asked.

"Nothing so useful as your work," Goewin answered.

"Lleu has been repairing the mosaics," I said, running my hands over the cooling gate. It felt even more beautiful to touch than it was to see, rougher and more textured than a knife blade, but not harsh.

"You need to learn a trade," Marcus said to Lleu solemnly, and Goewin and Gofan laughed.

Lleu said with cold dignity, "I am learning to use a sword."

"That's right," Gofan said in his deep voice, a gentle counter to the well-intentioned insolence of his pupil. "You need to be skilled in what's expected of you. How old are you—fifteen? If you were not the high king's son you would be apprenticed by now, or starting to be. But you aren't expected to learn a craft beyond the soldiery and husbandry you are already being taught. Your art and skill must lie in leadership."

Goewin said, straightfaced, "But is leadership something that can be taught?"

"I'll always have people like you about to make sure what I want will be done," Lleu said comfortably.

The iron under my hands steadied me; minutes ago it had been crimson with heat, molten, but was no longer.

"I won't pave your floors," Marcus said.

"Oh many thanks, my loyal servant," Lleu said, folding his arms. "I wouldn't ask it of you."

"This gate we are making is no more necessary and serves no greater purpose than the mosaic he has been mending," Gofan corrected his apprentice. "I am doing this because I enjoy the work; and Medraut enjoys watching us, and when the gate is finished others will enjoy seeing it and using it. Someone put as much pride and thought into the villa's tiled floor, and Lleu is doing an honorable thing in preserving that creation."

As though he felt it was his duty to undercut his master's

point, Marcus said, "Do you know what is happening in the lower mines right now?"

I looked up from the smooth metal.

"What is happening?" Goewin asked.

Marcus, having introduced the subject, apparently felt he had said as much as was required of him. After he had rested in self-satisfied silence for a moment or two, I explained, "There's been so much rain that the lowest level is flooded. The bedrock stops the water from sinking into the ground, and we have to keep emptying water out."

Lleu began, "I could be—"

"You couldn't be," Goewin told him. "You could never be a miner—no more than you could be a plowman or a weaver."

"What can I be?"

All arrogance crushed, Lleu slid from the sill where he was sitting and stepped into the muddy, sunlit yard to look at the sky. I followed him and stood next to him, looking not at the sky but at the bare red Edge and the black leafless trees that lined it. "Medraut, you belong here," Lleu said.

Imagine my surprise. I answered gently, "You were born here."

"But I don't belong. Even if I owned it all—you know your way through the mines, over the moors. How? I barely know my way across the Edge."

"Nonsense," I said. "You are learning. You recognize the malachite we mine for copper, and you know we use it to make bronze; you use it in the mosaics in another way."

Lleu considered the low, quick-scudding clouds, listening but apparently nonchalant. "I wish I had made those

51

mosaics," he said. "I know they aren't perfect; you can see the mistakes, the wrong colors in places, uneven lines in the borders. But who does such work anymore, now that the Romans are gone? I wish I could see the pattern books they used. And the work of other artists, and other kinds of artistry. I wish I had seen the paintings that were on the walls before Father rebuilt the house."

I was both amused and curiously saddened by his outburst. "You will have to travel," I said lightly. "In Byzantium there are mosaics and frescoes to fill your thirsty heart brim full. Today content yourself with Gofan's iron gates."

"I would, but Marcus makes me feel an idiot. 'You need to learn a trade'!" he mimicked with some fire.

I laughed. "You are neither an engineer nor a warrior like your father, but you have your own artistry. In time you'll dance circles around an argument, just as now you turn aside your opponent's blade."

He did not answer, but he thought on it. Then he turned and went back inside. I stood alone in the dooryard, half smiling to think how absurd this was, that I should be working to convince Lleu of his worth.

So the year was gone. In the spring Artos made Lleu the heir to his kingdom, naming him prince of Britain. In a year Lleu had changed from a weakling child to a matchless swordsman, the moth hatched from the worm at last; I must be dull in his shadow, shotten, mean. I had come here sick with the power I had known in the Orcades as your counselor and aide and executioner, and I ought now to be content with my newfound quiet authority. Lleu's own triumph should not matter. But it did matter. Standing in the Lesser

Hall among the high king's Comrades with Goewin at my side, waiting at first light in tense silence for the meeting to begin—it mattered; though outwardly I was all serene control, shut and screened behind my eyes. And Goewin shored me. She and Ginevra were the only women present, but since Ginevra stood at her husband's side as his queen, Goewin was alone. She seemed shorter than she was, dwarfed by Caius the steward at her right hand. Nothing softened her hard expression.

Lleu confronted the assembled crowd white-faced, but appearing strangely elegant; he stood slight and straight before his father, dressed simply and bearing no arms, his dark hair clipped short in the old style of a Roman soldier. He listened gravely as the high king informed him of the duties that were to be expected of him. Then Ginevra armed him, as had his namesake's mother, binding to his side a real sword; and at last the king presented his youngest child, his heir, to the strong, watchful company of his Comrades. Lleu bowed to us and pledged us his loyalty and service, and one by one we pledged ourselves to him. As my turn finished, Caius began to speak, passing over Goewin. I reached across her and silenced him gently with a gesture, and said only, "Princess?"

Repeating the words that I had used, she too pledged her loyalty to her twin: "Lleu son of Artos, my prince and brother, I swear to you my life and my allegiance."

Lleu watched her with sympathetic eyes, and let his solemn lips twitch into a smile before her turn passed. At my side, unnoticed by anyone else, Goewin slipped her cool fingers into my hand and pressed it gratefully.

After the pledges were finished Artos crowned his son with a thin fillet of gold and declared him prince of Britain.

When the ceremony was over Goewin hid herself, disappearing as quietly and completely as this season's infant bats asleep in the box hung under the eaves. I found her in the dark end of the porch, where the old, disused masonry and broken columns lie piled out of the way, waiting patiently for the rest of the villa to catch up to them in decay. Goewin huddled against the far wall behind the last pillars, sobbing passionately. Embarrassed and ashamed to see me, she hid her face in the hem of her smock and mumbled incoherently, "The Romans have gone from Britain forever."

I said gently, "Goewin. Come here." I led her out into the garden, and stood with a hand on her shoulder, as I had stood by Lleu not long before. "What do you mean?"

"Father's kingdom, this unity, it won't last—Lleu's not like him, and even if he were, too much is changing too fast. It can't last. Father would have me marry Constantius, the son of the king of Dumnonia in the south. It won't be bad, it's important, with all the tin mines and fishing towns. But he may as well marry me to one of my cousins and exile me to the Orcades, as he has his sister, because you can be sure I won't sit by as queen of Dumnonia and watch Britain trickle through Lleu's fingers. If I have to I'll take the kingship from him by force."

"Princess!" I exclaimed.

"If you don't destroy him first," she finished. "I hate living at the end of things!"

"Look." I pointed toward Elder Field. We gazed across the fields to the trees growing on the Edge, bright green with young leaves. The red stone of the bare cliff was fierce and strong and joyful in the spring sun, and two magpies sat preening themselves on the grass verge before the wall at the bottom of the garden. "There is no end," I said. "Only the beginning of something else."

V

Sparring

A month later this isolate, close-woven world of mine was shattered. That evening the peacocks were calling as I walked home from the Edge, their weird screeches scoring the long summer afternoon, and I was unaware of them. The sound was too familiar, a noise I had long ago learned not to hear. But Ginevra does not keep peacocks. I stepped onto the colonnade to join the family in the Queen's Garden, where we rested through the late sunsets, and stopped, struck through with a stunned, wintry surprise that felt something like despair. Smiling, you rose and crossed the garden to where I stood, and clasped my hands in greeting.

I stood trapped, desperate and ridiculous, trying to find the sense in why you were here. Finally I thought of your younger children, King Lot's children, and remembered that Artos had recently sent for them at my own suggestion to raise in his court. I had not ever considered that you might come with them. While I stood staring hopelessly you echoed my silence: your lean fingers closed firmly around mine, your blank eyes like fields of slate the perfect reflection of my own. Mother and son, flame and shadow, image and opposite—witless I stood before you and let them all see how alike we are.

At last I said quietly, "Godmother," and walked down the few steps into the garden with you.

Ginevra called to me to sit by her, and I swiftly accepted her invitation; you watched me with amusement and said, "So, my child, you have found your place here just as you left it?"

Oh, God, they were all staring at me—Lleu at his mother's feet stopped fiddling with his sandal straps, and your own four boys gazed with unabashed curiosity. Even Goewin watched intently from her perch on one of the low stone ledges, knees drawn up and chin resting on bare arms. And Artos, my father, bored through my patent desolation with ruthless scrutiny. "Very much the same, my lady," I tried to answer calmly, but my renegade hands clenched and unclenched as though in anger or fear.

Ginevra said, "It's good to have him back among us. Lleu owes his life to Medraut's skill."

You smiled and answered, "I am glad," and turned your smoky gaze on Lleu. He smiled back hesitantly, nervous fingers twitching at the sandal thongs again. My heart surged with jealousy and fear: and all you did was to look at him.

You sat down again. The boys clustered at your shoulders, uncertain as to what was expected of them. "Sit down, lads," Ginevra said gently. "Be at ease."

Well schooled in how to respond to the queen of Britain,

they obediently found places for themselves. Gwalchmei and Gaheris competed with good nature for space on the ledge opposite Goewin; young Gareth sat shyly next to Lleu as though offering tentative friendship. Only Agravain remained standing by your shoulder, his long copper hair so like yours, his mouth set in obstinate, defensive pride. Silently, stubbornly, he insisted on allegiance to you.

You appear ever serene to unfamiliar eyes. To see you, no one could have guessed you had been traveling for weeks; but you had not been in the garden long, and I realized you had only just then been introduced to the prince and princess. Gazing still at Lleu, you addressed him suddenly: "Lleu son of Artos, Lleu the son of the Dragon, the youngest child of the high king. And luckiest! Bright One, Fair One, and now prince of Britain."

At this spate of names and titles Lleu stopped fidgeting and straightened. "My lady? Aunt, Queen Morgause?" he answered boldly.

"How proud and brave you are"—you smiled—"for one so slight, so young. I would have my children pledge you their loyalty as have the rest of the high king's Comrades."

"There will be time for that," Ginevra said, with a sharp glance at Artos.

He finished her thought, ignoring any web you might attempt to weave. "Let them at least speak to each other first."

"Have your boys seen the estate yet?" I asked, and when you answered that they had not, I said quickly, "Then let me show them." For I could not sit at ease with you in the garden.

The twins came as well, and with your four children we walked over the grounds of the estate. Lleu and Goewin, merely by doing what was expected of them and acting with friendly courtesy, quickly gained the devotion of their two younger cousins; for Gaheris is rarely treated with courtesy, and Gareth is easy to like. Not so with Agravain, the jealous one, the dour one. He is a few years older than Lleu and Goewin, but not, as is Gwalchmei, old or wise enough for the twins to feel they must respect him. So, your four children were subject now to the careless arrogance of the prince of Britain, who could not keep straight their names.

The villa was by that summer restored and intact. The windows were clear and clean, and the mosaics awash with light even on cloudy days. The drought and famine were as well as forgotten. Here was wealth, and ancient splendor, artistry and perfection. Beneath Gofan's curious wrought-iron lampstands, the cushions of the low couches in the atrium were bright and luxurious in the sunlight, and the air was fresh with the green scent of the little lemon trees that Ginevra had set about the spacious room. Your children stepped cautiously across the glinting floors, openly admiring. But they too are princes, and even in the Orcades enjoyed a certain degree of luxury; so after we had been through Caius's well-kept stables, Gwalchmei turned to Lleu as prince to prince and offered, "Would you like to see the animals Mother brought with her? They're supposed to be gifts for your father."

They were caged, of course, for the journey. There were small wildcats and highland deer, a monkey and a remarkable collection of birds. There were hawks and songbirds, and there were peacocks. "These could be let free to roam the grounds," Gwalchmei said. "If they're well fed they won't disturb your gardens, and they can't fly far."

"I've never seen a real one," Goewin said. "Mama has a mosaic of one with its tail spread on the floor of her chamber. Do they spread their tails?"

"Only when they feel like it," Agravain said, and Gareth added, "They're very conceited."

"Where did you get them?" Lleu asked.

"Mother sends for them. She always keeps peacocks," Gareth explained.

"They're beautiful," Lleu said, his attention fixed on the haughty birds, rapt.

"Mother will be pleased you like them," Gaheris ventured.

Agravain told him, "Mother didn't bring these for the prince." All their conversation ever referred back to you.

They were anxious to test Lleu's swordsmanship, and over the next week they organized several duels with him. Gwalchmei and I, and sometimes Goewin, would sit on the back wall of the estate as judges, kicking our heels against the dry stone; and on the grass lawn before us Gareth, Gaheris, and Agravain took turns trying to outwit Lleu, and failing. The two younger boys did not seem to mind and enjoyed the challenge and practice. But Agravain was not pleased at being consistently trounced by one younger and slighter than himself.

It chokes me to think of the day you happened upon us during one of these sessions. Agravain could hardly bear for you to watch, and even Gareth began to feel the derision in your gaze. Finally, resting from his last bout, Gaheris asked Lleu, "Could you take on two of us at once?"

"All right," Lleu said.

"No. Three of us," Agravain demanded harshly.

"That's not fair!" said Goewin.

"I'll do it," Lleu said amiably.

Only Gareth was dubious. "She's right."

"I'll take on as many as you like," Lleu said carelessly, and turned to Agravain to ask, "You do want me beaten, don't you?"

"No, my lord," Agravain said in blushing apology, caught, while you laughed quietly. "I only thought to test your skill."

"I won't fight three against one," Gareth said.

"Oh, come on," Lleu coaxed, confident. "It's only in play."

"It's not fair," said Gareth.

Agravain argued, "If it's all right with Lleu, then it's fair. If Gareth won't do it, Gwalchmei can."

"I won't do it, either," Gwalchmei said mildly. Artos had already made him one of the Comrades; he had no need to prove himself. "You will have to fend for yourselves."

"Medraut," you said suddenly. "You join them."

"What do you mean, Godmother?" I asked, chilly.

"I'd like to see how your skill compares to the prince's," you said.

And I must answer, "He can best me."

"Oh, Medraut, join us," Lleu said. "Just this once. It's only a game."

"Join them," you said. It was a command.

I said in a low voice, "Godmother, I would rather not."

61

"Don't glare so," you said coolly. "Join them."

Helpless as I was before you always, I had no choice but to obey. In fierce silence I took up one of the wooden swords, and with Gaheris and Agravain took my place opposite Lleu.

He eluded us, foxlike, avoiding and repelling our blows. We might as well try to fight a waterfall. He disarmed Gaheris again and again, and Gaheris admitted defeat when Gwalchmei called out to him, "You're finished. If it were real swords you'd be dead by now." And with Gaheris out, Agravain, Lleu, and I were suddenly pitted against one another in earnest, and playing a little desperately.

But Lleu fought me as though we were the only two people in the world. He dealt with Agravain because he had to, fending off his cousin's blows as though Agravain were no more annoying than an insect, a trifling interruption. Agravain fought doggedly, retrieving his sword twice from the ground, growing more and more irritable. The third time Agravain's sword went flying across the grass, Lleu stamped furiously on the wooden hilt so that it splintered and cracked before Agravain could pick it up again. Agravain snatched hold of Lleu's arm, trying to pull him down with his hands.

"Let go!" Lleu cried in a high voice, and when Agravain did not, Lleu suddenly and unexpectedly tumbled to the ground and rolled out of his reach.

"Get out of there," Goewin shouted. "He's beaten you."

Agravain tossed his long, burnished braid pridefully over his shoulder and came away, to slump in silent anger next to his brothers against the stone wall.

Then it was Lleu and I, alone, locked together in silent, furious intensity. The old bitter resentment raged through me: I was stronger and taller and more experienced than Lleu, and I knew I could not win. He must defeat me before you and all your young sons. I fought with passionate disregard for our difference in size, knowing he was my better, and that my strength was my only advantage. But Lleu slipped out of my range, dodged my blows and parried with a ferocity and determination fully equal to my attack. When Lleu at last twisted in underneath my guard and pressed the wooden blade against my throat, I could not bear to prolong this competition. I knelt before him in formal surrender, as before a judge or an executioner, with head bowed and neck bared.

"Oh, well done!" Gareth breathed.

"Well done," you echoed.

Lleu let fall his sword. He offered me his hand to help me rise; I took it and got slowly to my feet. Such a performance, both of us so calm and polite! But his hands trembled, the black hair he pushed back from his forehead was damp, and his face was wan. It had been something more than a game.

VI
The Running of the Deer

I do not like the sword. It is clumsy and imprecise, designed for haphazard damage, for total and purposeless destruction. With bow and arrow the kill is clean and swift: That is the weapon of the hunter, not the warrior, the one who kills beast, not man, who kills for survival, not power. Try bringing down a hart, or a hare, or a swan, with a sword.

I tell this over to myself as a litany, so to excuse the delight I draw from the chase, the exhilaration and abandon that Lleu calls bloodthirst. After you came to Camlan, to hunt was all my solace or pleasure. I most often went alone, at my ease in the deep, green forest south of Camlan, not even expected to return at night those times I was not needed in the mines. On days when I must work I could at least stalk rabbit and partridge through the twisted trees clinging to the red sandstone of the Edge. I carried a bow with me always, those days.

So it was one morning when Goewin came to my room early and asked, "Will you be hunting on the Edge today?" She knew, as all Camlan knew, how I passed my spare hours.

"I had not meant to," I answered briefly, my hands busy with knife and horn and bowstring. "Why?"

"Lleu and the cousins are planning to play some kind of game there," she said, sitting at my desk and watching me stock my quiver. "They'll be all over chasing and hiding from each other. I think they're a lot of idiots, but I wouldn't want you to mistake one of them for a wild pig and stick an arrow through somebody's throat."

That made me laugh. "What are they doing that you aren't with them?"

"They're playing out a hunt. Not a real one. They'll take some hounds, but no bows or spears."

She was still frowning. I asked, "What are they hunting, then, that you so fiercely disapprove?"

With the tip of a finger the gentle princess crushed a small and shining insect that was moving across my desk, and flicked it through the open window. "Lleu."

"I hope he proves a better quarry than he is a hunter," I said.

She gave a short, explosive gasp of laughter. "Oh! Well, he knows the Edge better than the cousins do. He can hide from them even if he can't outrun them. That's why they need the hounds." She stood up to leave, and finished, "I just wanted to warn you."

"Thank you," I said.

But she waited at the door and did not go. "If Lleu

escapes them and returns to the Queen's Garden by sunset without being caught, he wins. I won't join in something so childish. The prince of Britain!" She paused. "Oh, well."

"Childish, no," I said. "Not the Wild Hunt."

Goewin laughed. "Gwyn-ap-Nudd hounding the souls of the dead across the sky? Morgause's children aren't that bad."

"No." I laughed with her. "But in the south they used to play out the Wild Hunt in earnest, ending with the chosen victim ritually slaughtered on his own threshold. They still do it in some places, only now the killing is mimicked."

"God help us," Goewin said grimly. "I hope our fair cousins don't know about that."

"I don't think so."

"It's as well you're not playing," she said as she turned to go. I stood looking after her with bow in hand, thinking that to follow Lleu would be sport indeed. And then the thought, Why should I not? I would not interrupt his game; but I would watch.

I challenged myself to guess what Lleu would do. His cousins must let him start first, so that he might have an initial hope of eluding them; I thought he might head south on the track through the beech woods that leads to the fisheries. The forest there was heavy with the heat of August, sunlight filtering green and gold through the thick leaves. I tethered my horse well off the track where it was screened by dark rhododendron, and then I hid among the ferns to watch for Lleu. To lie there was pleasant, knowing that I waited only for my brother, and that I need not be alert for a chase. The loam forest floor was cool against my chest and palms, piebald with spots of sunlight that were hot on my back. And as I lay half dreaming so, a doe stepped from the tall undergrowth across the path, and presently another joined it. I lay breathing the warm scent of fern, my mind empty of anything but the grazing deer, for what seemed a measureless space of time.

Lleu appeared at last, moving easily and almost noiselessly along the path, listening and careful. He wore short leather trousers and a linen shirt, and seemed somehow to be only another kind of wild forest creature. He did not even carry a hunting knife. He stopped when he saw the deer, as still as I, and watched. They might have even been aware of him, but did not run. My left hand lay across the shaft of my bow, but still; I closed the fingers of my right hand upon a small twig, and threw it gently past the head of the closer deer. Both their heads went up; they eyed Lleu a brief moment in recognition of his unwanted presence, and then bolted back into the forest. Lleu called softly after them: "Run swiftly, sisters."

I watched him pass and let him go. Then I got to my feet, bound my hair out of my face, and went back to the horse. I waited long enough to give Lleu a fair edge, then followed after him. Oh, he moves lightly enough, but at first it was not difficult to track him; he could not help but leave an occasional sandal print in the soft earth, or at least broken branches and trampled ferns. Yet I lost him. He passed the fisheries and came back indirectly, familiar and more at ease on his own ground than I had expected. The southern end of the lake is grown over with spindly trees and dense reeds; the land there becomes marshy and uncertain. By moving quickly from clump of grass to hummock of turf it is possible to make one's way to the island in the center of the lake, though it appears unattainable from the shore. Cautiously and quietly, Lleu must have picked his way through the bog until he reached the firm ground of the island. Once there, he could lie flat underneath the thorny blackberry canes and wait till sunset, gazing at the sky through the tangle of briars and green leaves, listening to the marsh birds calling and insects humming. I thought with scorn, Easy enough to outwit his cousins if he chooses to hide on Glass Island all day. So I turned my attention back to the forest and to my own hunting, and left Lleu to his vigil.

I had an easy day. I rode slowly, lulled by solitude and the stillness of the forest. I saw no more deer, and though I caught two small partridges, the day seemed to be passing without incident. I struck back toward Elder Field and was nearing the foot of the bare stone cliff that is the highest point of the Edge when I heard Agravain's voice raised in a shout of discovery, followed by the unmistakable pandemonium of dogs chasing through thick woodland. I rode toward the noise, drawn. When I came nearer, I found Lleu engaged in a heated confrontation at the bottom of the cliff: Agravain and Gaheris had caught him, and Agravain was holding him pinned against the red stone, though as I watched Lleu managed to wrench himself out of his cousin's grip. But he was cornered. Unable to go anywhere else, surely without thinking, he began to climb the cliffside.

Agravain half tore one of the sleeves from Lleu's shirt in his effort to pull him back; but Lleu kicked downward at him sharply, striking him on the chin and then the shoulder. Agravain fell backward and slid, but Lleu still climbed, finding footholds and handholds instinctively. He must be tearing his palms to shreds, but he was startlingly secure on the cliff face. And Agravain, sportsman that he is, snatched up a stone the size of an egg and hurled it at Lleu. He missed, but came deadly close, and the rock wall next to one of Lleu's feet crumbled away in sharp spalls and shards of stone. Lleu yelled, "Don't—no!" He shouted a name at random.

His cousin let fly another missile and roared, "*Agravain!* Learn it, you pompous imbecile!"

Rock slammed into the cliffside inches from one of Lleu's hands. He clung to cracks in the sheer sandstone, thirty feet above the ground, and cried, "Agravain, stop it!"

Gaheris made a feeble attempt to restrain his brother, but Agravain shook him off. I swung down from my horse and caught hold of Agravain's arm even as he drew it back for a third shot. He turned in fury, but went scarlet and shamefaced when he saw who halted him. Lleu, above us, could do nothing but continue climbing. He gained a narrow ledge halfway up the cliff, barely as wide as his body, and hauled himself along it till he lay with his face turned to the rock wall.

"What should I do?" Agravain stammered in dismay, searching my face for guidance.

"Think," I said, and let go of his wrist. He and Gaheris stood silent for a moment or two, flushed with embarrassment. At last Agravain called to Lleu, "My lord, you're not hurt?"

Lleu looked down. Agravain stuttered on, "My lord, I'm sorry—I didn't think. You'd kicked me—I was too angry to think. You're not hurt, are you?" I managed not to laugh at his clumsy apology.

"I'm fine," Lleu said slowly. "No, I'm not hurt. Well met, Medraut."

"The pleasure is mine," I answered spontaneously.

"Prince—," Gaheris began uncertainly, and Agravain said again, "My lord—"

Their formal humility seemed to steady Lleu. "It's all right," he said; and paused for a moment, then added sharply, "But, Gaheris, you might act with a little more speed and assurance next time. And you, Agravain: Stop to think." His mastery of their names was suddenly flawless.

"Yes, my lord," Gaheris said in a low voice. Agravain said nothing. He winced as though he had been struck.

"Never mind now," Lleu said. "Begin again." He lowered himself off the ledge and spidered sideways until he reached more level ground. I made certain that Agravain and Gaheris gave their cousin a period of grace in which to get clear of them, their forfeit for such stupidity. Lleu ran east, toward home; we waited till the leaves quivering behind him were still, then left each other.

It was hot. After I was alone once more the afternoon was silent, the gold-gilt air heavy and humming with insects. I too rode eastward, but this time without any real aim. I let the horse pick its own way along the sandstone screes. The rowan was ripening in handfuls of flaming orange, and early blackberries were beginning to cluster among the white flowers. In the shade of dark holly leaves I came upon the stone trough of the Holy Well and stopped to drink and dash spring water over my face and hair. Then, as I stood and let the cold run down my back, on the hillside below I caught the unmistakable flash of tall red flank and broad spreading antler. Stillness and drowsiness fell away, and I turned with all my being to the hunt, and a quarry equal to my pursuit.

Plunging heedless through briar and sharp, rattling holly, I set my horse racing down the hillside after the stag. It could not shake me; I had done so little all day that the horse was still fresh. Low on the Edge, where the underbrush goes from scrub trees to dense fern, I began to close in. Then, unexpectedly, the stag veered to avoid a slight, dark figure that appeared without warning ahead of it. Now, of all moments, Lleu crossed my path: he stumbled to his feet from the ferns where he had thrown himself to avoid being trampled by the stag pursued, then crashed back down on one knee as I followed hard upon the stag. And this time he would have been crushed but for my own desperate and lightning drag on the reins, which nearly threw me as the horse abruptly turned from the track and stopped short.

Blind anger coursed through me for a moment. We were both suddenly frustrated—I had lost my prey, Lleu had his path blocked. He knelt frozen on one knee, ragged, unaccountably barefoot, filthy and torn; I sat my dancing, snorting horse with bow in hand. Lleu's eyes had the mute and desperate look of a hunted creature in flight. Of course: I remembered the game. And so I shaped my vengeance for the loss of a deer, and for Lleu's wooden sword held at my throat. I said hoarsely, "You're quarry still?"

He nodded, speechless.

"Then I've lost none," I said, and let fly an arrow to tear through a dangling shred of his sleeve. It caught there, and hung.

He stared at it in astonishment, then reached one hand to pull it free and put the other hand down to push himself upright. And straight I set another arrow quivering in the ground in the inch of space between his fingers and his bare foot.

This was an even better challenge than the stag, and more dangerous. I concentrated my entire being on my hands, aware that I must strike with perfect and absolute precision.

"Don't move," I said.

Lleu did not move. He crouched there, almost under the hooves of my horse, and I sent another arrow skimming over his hair. Wild-eyed, he cried in a whisper, "If you should miss!"

"I don't!" I cried back at him, and shot another arrow past his head that went so close the fletching grazed his ear. "I never miss!"

"Stop shooting at me!" Lleu screamed. He watched me fit another arrow to my bow and sobbed, "You're wasting arrows!"

I shot into the arch his forefinger and thumb made where they rested against the ground. "It's worth it," I said fervently, and pulled another arrow from my quiver. Still and white as a statue of alabaster, Lleu hissed wordlessly at me through clenched teeth, like a cat.

It made me drop the arrow with a shout of laughter. "Hunter turns quarry," I gasped, unable to stop laughing, "man turns beast. Get up, you idiot."

Lleu rose slowly. Two arrows stood in the earth between his bare, dusty, scratched feet, and a third hung from his torn sleeve. "I won't run from you," he said in a low voice. "I don't care if they do catch me. But I won't let you think you frighten me."

"If you could see how white you are," I said weakly, wiping my eyes with the back of one hand.

"It's not so funny," he said through his teeth. "It's not funny at all."

"I apologize for laughing then," I said. "I haven't laughed as much in years."

"If ever," Lleu said stonily. His color was returning, and anger replacing fear.

"Why did you leave Glass Island?" I asked.

"I was bored, and it seemed like cheating—no one had any idea where I was." He stared at me. "You tracked me *there*? Then you have been—" He stopped, and repeated fiercely, "I won't run from you."

I said, "Little lord, I won't make you run from me. You can run from your cousins." Then I raised my hunting horn and sounded a long call. "Are you fit enough to outrun them all the way to Camlan?"

"Damn you!" Lleu cried. "Damn you, Medraut! I've been running all afternoon!" He pushed past my horse, but after going several paces turned back to look at me. I laughed and blew another horn call. He tore down the slope away from me.

I followed in his wake at a leisurely pace, triumphant and exhausted by the terrible hairline precision of those five wasted arrows. What did it matter to me if Lleu managed to reach the Queen's Garden ahead of his cousins? He did outrun them, after all: he must. He was fully aware that he had lost to me and was determined not to lose to them.

The game should have ended there.

But during the course of the day Lleu had left his youngest cousin bound hand and foot somewhere on the Edge, and, thoughtless idiot that he was, he had forgotten. Gareth is best natured of any of your boys, and when we found him he considered himself to have been fairly beaten; this despite having been trussed up all afternoon with Lleu's sandal straps.

You were not so forgiving.

That evening at supper all four of your boys were still talking of the day's game, and you listened to them with amused and indulgent laughter. But as we were rising to leave the meal you drew Lleu aside and said to him softly, "But, my prince, you won't be so neglectful of my youngest child again, will you?"

"Of course not, my lady," Lleu said readily. "Gareth wasn't ever in any danger, though. I left the dogs to guard him." He added, "I did apologize to him after. I'll apologize to you, if you like."

And you to him: "Perhaps you ought to be punished."

"That is for my father to decide," Lleu answered, purposefully regal, "not you, Aunt."

"I will suggest it to your father," you said directly to Lleu, though Artos himself sat by, watching your performance with silent contempt.

"I will consider it when you do," Artos said, rising slowly and standing poised with one hand on the table, like a wary forest creature gauging a potential enemy. "Punishment and revenge are two different things." You held Lleu with one hand on his shoulder and he stood still, waiting for you to release him.

I do not trust your nails so close to anyone's eyes, and with a sudden, abrupt movement I freed Lleu from your hold. Ginevra spoke curtly, voicing my thought: "Don't touch him."

You turned to me and laid a hand against my own cheek in Lleu's stead. A gentle, tender touch, and I thought it to be mocking. "Or me," I said, turning your hand aside. You smiled at Lleu mildly and said, "An apology is not always enough. But never mind, this time."

VII

The Queen of the Orcades

The following day it rained, but a few of us still sat on the colonnade after supper rather than in the atrium. The evening was warm and light, the stone and tile porch a pleasant place to sit and breathe the rich, fresh smell of the wet gardens rising around. Artos and I played draughts, and between us Goewin concentrated on the moves we made. It should have been a quiet interim of rest. But you came out to the colonnade to join us; you stopped behind me to examine the game, and as you stood there you brushed the tips of your fingers against the back of my neck. Such a curious thrill of mixed delight and repulsion ran through my body that my arms broke out in gooseflesh. Instinctively I tried to cringe beyond your reach. Artos said to you mildly, "You're interrupting."

"Oh, I can find better sport than this," you said lightly, and sat behind Artos on a chair by the edge of the porch.

When Lleu came out a few minutes later you called to him, "Stay with me. Speak to me," and he was too polite and not enough in awe of you to think to do otherwise. "You're cold," you said to him in a normal voice. "Talk to me, and I will chafe your hands." Lleu sat on the tiles at your feet, and let you breathe on his hands and rub them gently as the two of you spoke together. I bent scowling over the patterned board as though I could not see you.

But your idle chatter ceased after a time, and at last Goewin attracted my attention with a scant, quiet gesture of one finger. Lleu was asleep: sleeping just as he had been sitting, on the floor at your feet, leaning with his head propped against your knee and one hand still resting in your lap. As I watched, you moved a thin hand to wander over his hair. When you noticed my slow glance you clasped Lleu's hand firmly between your own, mocking, challenging, tempting. The playing piece I was holding suddenly snapped between my fingers.

Steadily I set the broken pieces on the board before me and rose from my seat, while Artos swung around on his stool to see what it was that so intrigued me. I bent to you and whispered past your ear, "What can you possibly want of Lleu?"

You smiled, unruffled. "What do you mean?"

I whispered in anger: "You are unusually affectionate."

You laughed outright. When you spoke your words were directed at me, but your voice was pitched to include Artos and Goewin. "Here and now you scorn my affection, though when you were small you too crept to me for comfort after I had you whipped."

I snapped, "What has that to do with Lleu?" and then

tried hard to check my anger. I stood looking down at you with my hands resting unclenched on my hips. "You have not had the prince whipped, and he has not crept to you for comfort."

"Has he not?" you said, ruffling Lleu's hair. "My company must be uninteresting; I seem to have put him to sleep." You looked toward Goewin and Artos, and said, "Medraut has not changed. Even as a child he found me suspect, always contradicting me, stubbornly at odds with me. He seemed to dare me to be strict with him. I sometimes had to have him punished for things Gwalchmei had done."

"I only regret you were burdened with such a child for so long," Artos said coldly. "I would have sent for him sooner if I had known."

"Once he was beaten so severely that he was burning with fever when he came to me," you continued relentlessly. "It was because he had accused me of lying. Do you remember, Medraut? You were only ten."

"I was seven," I said through my teeth, quietly.

You shrugged. "No matter. Young enough. But even then you would not admit afterward that you were wrong."

I rapped out in exasperation, "Who cares what I did? It was almost twenty years ago."

"Two years ago you were even more abject before me," you said, gently stroking my damaged hand. "And still are, I think." You took hold of the scarred fingers and kissed them.

I pulled myself free and choked, "You will *not*—"; but I broke away without finishing and turned to walk heavily down the stone steps into the rain and the dripping gardens.

I will never go back again, I thought, I will never again go creeping back to beg for your forgiving hands on my hair.

I walked blindly away from the house and stopped at the stone wall on the edge of the estate, facing away and toward the hills. There I stood shaking with anguished, angry sobs, hardly aware that I was driving my knuckles so fiercely against the wet stone that I was tearing the skin.

Goewin followed me. She stood next to me for a long time, leaning against the wall without speaking, waiting for me to grow calmer. Finally she laid her own hand over my blighted fingers, and said, "She can't control you now."

"She can," I gasped, "she can. Oh, God, I wish she'd never come. Why doesn't she leave?"

"Why should she?" Goewin said reasonably. "She may never see her boys again. She talks idly, and stirs evil memories, but she is powerless here."

I turned to look at her, measuring her with my eyes. She watched me, worried, wondering. Even then I was afraid to tell her, to tell anyone, but I must confide in someone or go mad. I said at last, "It was she who ruined my hand. The fingers were broken in a hunt, as I told you, and she was called in to set the bones. She twisted and broke them beyond repair, on purpose. Later they had to be broken again. I reset them myself."

"Why?" Goewin breathed in soft disbelief. "Why would anyone do such a thing?"

"To teach me a lesson, just as she said," I spat. "To teach me not to break all my bones hunting. God help me, she was so angry—they carried me in torn and broken, flesh bled white, filthy with dust and stinking with stag's blood. She was so angry. She cursed me for an idiot under her breath all the while she was mending the splintered bones in my legs and wrist."

"Medraut, I have seen you hunt," Goewin whispered. "Why would you let yourself be so terribly hurt?"

"We were on foot, with spears, and I went against a full-grown stag with my dagger," I answered, knowing that such a response explained nothing. "That she should fondle Lleu's hands like that, all the while thinking of what she has done to mine! She is so unpredictable, and so cruel—"

"She hasn't hurt us," Goewin said.

"And so strong," I finished, pushing the wet hair back from my face. "Even after she destroyed my hand I still clutched at her for comfort, just as I did as a child. I went back to her, trembling, every time."

"But why should you be so afraid of her?" Goewin persisted.

"When I resist her she invokes our dark secret, that she is my mother, and I must obey."

"Is it so secret?" Goewin asked. "You call her Godmother."

"No one knows. Only those few who were sworn to silence at the time of my birth, and now you and Lleu. It is why Artos would never make me his heir, even if I were his only child. There is nothing I count more shameful. I could not bear for her other children to know."

"But *why,* Medraut?" Goewin insisted quietly.

"What do you think?" I replied in equal quiet.

She looked away. She wanted a straight answer, and I would not give her one. "Tell me what you think," I repeated. "You have heard me talking in my sleep, you have seen the scars across my back. Surely you have made a guess."

"All right," she said in grim determination. She still pressed her hand over mine, trusting and intimate and infinitely courageous. "This is what I have guessed, Medraut. I think that you were like all the rest of us, ignorant of your parentage, and that you and Morgause were lovers. And when you found out she is your mother you set out to destroy yourself."

I said nothing. Goewin asked at length, "Is that right?"

"No," I answered bitterly. "You could hardly think worse of me! But you're wrong. I have always known she is my mother."

Goewin stared at the wall, her jaw set, frowning. We were both drenched through. "She has no power here," Goewin said at last with stubborn certainty, to reassure herself as well as me. "You told her so much yourself. Lleu wasn't punished. She can do nothing."

"I lack your courage before her," I said. "I have brought down a king of stags with my bare hands and a hunting knife, but she can bring me down with a few words and an idle kiss." Once more I pushed damp hair out of my eyes, and smiled ruefully. "Ah, God, I'm dripping wet."

Goewin smiled with me. "I too. Come back inside." Calm now, we walked up through the silver and green and gray gardens. The colonnade was empty.

We met you in the hall. The lamps were not yet lit, and in the half-light of rain and evening it was too dark to see your face. "The prince is gone to bed," you told us softly. "You might step in and see that all is well; he is very cold, and Artos had to carry him in because we could not wake him."

"Could not wake him?" Goewin echoed in alarm.

"I would guess hemlock poisoning," you said seriously, "if I did not think better of my brother's servants."

Goewin said in disgust, "Who would do such a thing? He

must have a fever." She pushed past you toward Lleu's bedroom, but I did not follow immediately. I asked you quietly, in the old routine, "What kind of fever makes one shiver?"

"You need not be afraid," you said. "I think he will recover by morning."

Lleu lay in bed, asleep. Goewin was drawing the tapestries across the windows when I came in, and Artos was lighting the brazier. I knelt by the bed and shook Lleu's shoulder, saying lightly, "What makes you so tired, little one?" He pushed my hand away halfheartedly and murmured a few unintelligible syllables, but he could not be roused enough to sit up or to say anything coherent. Nevertheless his breath was even, and he was not so very cold after all. Artos came to stand by my side; he asked quietly, "What is it?"

"Nothing, sir," I answered. Hemlock? Perhaps a thimbleful out of a poisoned cup, but not enough to harm him. It could have been accidental.

Then why should you think to suggest it?

I finished, "Nothing, except that he seems unusually tired. I think it will pass by morning."

"He's had no trouble breathing this year," Artos said, "and he is much stronger than he used to be. Medraut, your skill as a physician is equal to Aquila's; you're certain there's nothing the matter?"

"Nothing sleep won't cure. Truly, my lord," I answered.

We left it at that. During the next week the harvest began, and on days when I could help there I ate my meals in the open with the field-workers. Then I would return after dark, sunburned and exhausted, to fall into bed without speaking to anyone. Now even the mines frustrated me, for the shaft we were tunneling kept running into solid bedrock; we were unable to approach the vein of malachite that we felt sure was just beyond our reach. At the end of the week I sat at my desk, trying to draw up a plan for working around the bedrock, and I was too tired and too absorbed in my work to look up when Lleu came in.

"What's wrong with me?" he demanded. "You know. I'm sure you know. Are you drugging me?"

"No!" I turned my head sharply, facing him. I said in anger, "I swore to you! And why should I?"

"You don't dare lie to me," Lleu said fiercely.

"I'll dare anything," I told him, hearing my voice as quiet and deadly as I have ever heard yours. "But I don't lie."

We glared at one another in tense silence for a few moments. Then I sighed gently and propped my head against my hand, leaning on the desk and looking at him. "Am I to understand that you are still so tired?" I asked.

"Ever since the night after our game," he said. "Medraut, I'm sorry; but you know more about medicines and herbs than anyone else here."

Not so.

But he did not know of your skill, then, and I could scarcely believe you would risk your brother's wrath with such glaring treachery in his own house. I looked down at the dolphins of tile forever chasing each other across the sea-gray floor. "I have been working in the mines and in the fields every day this past fortnight," I said. "When would I find time to poison you? Why would I? God!"

"I'm sorry," he repeated softly, and almost on the verge of tears. "I'm sorry. But I'm afraid, Medraut! What is happening?"

"I can't say," I said slowly. "Is there anything besides the weariness?"

"Not really. But I just fall asleep! I'm not ill; it's like being drugged, it's like drinking poppy, or too much wine."

"Do you feel it now?"

"No," he admitted. "It comes and goes."

"Does anyone else know?" I asked.

"Only if they've noticed. I haven't told anyone but Goewin. Medraut, you have to do something; you can't just let me be mysteriously poisoned!"

"You do not know that it is poison," I said wearily, "and it may change. But I'll watch you. If you sense it starting again, come to me at once, or else send Goewin."

So he left, reassured. I thought of the things you had said that first night, and wondered, and wondered.

Goewin came for me just before dark, and early as it was I was already asleep. She shook my shoulder a little; though she rarely touched me at such times, for I slept naked beneath my blankets, and my nightmares disturbed her. And indeed, I was dreaming. Instead of waking, I snarled, "No!" and struck her full across the face.

She stood staring, not really hurt, but too astonished to speak. I sat upright in silence, tranced. "Sir?" she said tentatively, while I stared back at her without seeing her. "Medraut!"

"Princess?" I murmured finally, at last realizing where I was and what I had done. "Goewin?" We gaped at one another. "Forgive me. I—" I swallowed, shivering. "It was a dream, my lady. What do you want?"

She looked at me long and hard. At last she said slowly, "Something is wrong with Lleu. It's more than weariness; his wrists are chill as ice."

I listened with a still face, then swung out of bed and drew on a loose robe. I lit a candle and quietly searched my shelves for the vials I thought I would need. "Do you know what it is?" Goewin asked.

"I'm not sure," I said. "But if it is poison, it will be hemlock."

She pressed her lips together. "Can you help?"

"I think. Go, light a fire for him. I'll follow."

Goewin and I sat with Lleu late into the night, in part to comfort him, in part to minister to him, and in part to discuss together in low tones what was happening. More agitated than languid now, Lleu stirred the coals in the brazier and fidgeted restlessly with books and candlesticks, ornaments and games that lay about the room. He was unable to keep still. In the past two years he had reached his full stature and acquired a kind of wiry strength to match his natural grace; but now his gestures were determined and dogged, as though he had to concentrate and consider every movement he made. At last he sat on the floor next to the bed and for a moment collapsed with his face buried in his hands. Then he looked up and said, "Who is doing this?"

I think Goewin had some idea of the answer to that question, as I did. But neither of us spoke. "Can you guess? Do you know?" Lleu cried softly.

"I can guess," Goewin said with grim confidence.

"You can't lay blame for such a thing without proof," I said.

"We can tell Father and have him stop it."

"No!" I protested. "It may be accidental." I thought to make light of the threat, and to protect Lleu myself. "Think of the fear and anger that would spread through the estate if we spoke of poison. Lleu is not hurt."

"I am!" he said.

"You're not," I answered. "You're made uncomfortable, and you're frightened. But you aren't in danger."

Goewin argued in quiet fury, "How can you know? If it may be accidental, it may as easily be malicious, and because of your skill everyone will blame you, Medraut."

"I've already blamed you," Lleu put in quietly.

"Ai, Lleu, if you won't trust me, who will? It would shatter me to have you approach your father with such an accusation! I won't let any harm come to you."

"Medraut, I have never heard you so irrational!" Goewin cried. "All the food and drink in Camlan seems tainted when it reaches Lleu's lips."

"Then we'll get food for him from Elder Field," I said, uncompromising. "Please, Goewin, help me to see this through, help me to keep Camlan from ugly intrigue and suspicion."

I think that Goewin finally agreed because she so wanted me to prove to her that I was to be relied upon, that I would assure all would be well. Reluctantly, the twins did as I planned. Lleu came out to the fields with me and ate his meals there. The first morning at the reaping he bound a square of damp linen across his nose and mouth and said apologetically, "The dust makes it hard for me to breathe." But he worked as diligently as anyone else. Goewin shadowed him when he was at home, methodically and quietly making certain that he ate nothing from the house. Yet we remained on edge, not daring to trust that the matter could be finished.

VIII
A Game of Chess

Four days later we woke to find the Queen's Garden a riot of caged songbirds. It had been decorated before dawn at your whim and for your pleasure. Elegant cages of all different sizes and shapes stood on the walks and walls and hung from the little trees; colored ribbons and bells of bone and silver fluttered from the wicker bars. Ai, Godmother, how is it that for all your cruelty you have so keen an eye for beauty? It looked like a place for a wedding party.

You spent the day there, admiring the songbirds and feeding bread crumbs to the peacocks. Fascinated as a moth courting a candle flame, I came home from the fields early and wandered about beneath the graceful cages. I tried to stay apart from you; but the Queen's Garden is not very big. I forced myself at last to approach you where you sat on the grass among the peacocks, collecting the luminous and iridescent breast feathers that lay about. "When are you leaving?" I demanded.

You looked up with eyes the deep, sad gray or blue of a winter evening. "I will leave when the harvest is in," you said, pulling a stalk of lavender to strip the buds from it one by one, crushing them between your fingers until the air around your hands was sweet with their sharp scent. "I will go to Venta Belgarum to see my mother and then back to the Orcades.

"Only be patient," you added, stretching languid and cat-like. "It is so gentle and warm here. It reminds me of the Summer Country in the south, where I grew up. It is cold in the Orcades."

"Twenty miles to the east of here lie the High Peaks, and the country there is as cold and cruel as anything in the north," I said.

"Ah, but you like the cold." You brushed a peacock feather across my wrist and mourned, "Medraut, why did you not send me a pair of those beautiful African cats?"

"Oh, let be," I said mildly, and turned toward the house. Lleu was walking down the steps from the colonnade, looking about him in wonder. He too had left the fields early.

"No. Stay. Sit by me." You slipped your thin hand into mine to draw me down, and said conspiratorially, "I have been waiting for him. He'll like it, don't you think?"

Lleu made his way slowly from tower of hazel to palace of willow, slim brown hands brushing aside the snapping pennants, dark head bent or tilted skyward that he might mark each different bird. "I didn't come down here this morning," he called to you over his shoulder. "I only looked out through the atrium windows."

"Do you like it, Prince?" you asked.

He walked across to us slowly, looking about him with shining eyes. "It's lovely, Aunt!" he answered. "How did you think of it?"

"It's easy enough to think of entertainment when you are idle as I am," you said pleasantly. "Would you like me to tell you the names of the birds?"

"All right," he said, but continued his own slow tour of the garden. Finally he made his way back to us and held out his hands to you that he might help you rise. You took them gratefully, gracefully, peacock feathers fluttering from your fingers. But as you rose one of your fingernails tore a raw scrape across the inside of his wrist.

"Oh, pardon!" you exclaimed, snatching Lleu's hand to your lips so you might kiss the scratch.

He stood still and looked at you steadily. "My lady," he said in quiet, "what did you mean by that?"

"An accident only," you said.

"It was not an accident!" I cried, and made to stand. You halted me with one hand pressed to my shoulder, a silent order not to move. "Softer, my marksman, softer," you said. "I can hear you."

The breath of lavender hovered about your hand, and your red-and-black enameled bracelets clicked and clinked close to my ear. "You don't do anything by accident," I protested, but your hand on my shoulder held me powerless.

"Very rarely," you agreed. Lleu stood before you, shorter than you, slight and dark. The peacocks milled about his knees. "Why, Prince, you have gone pale as salt!" You laughed.

Lleu swiftly turned away from you. He diverted himself

as best he could, and ran his fingertips over the shining blue-black feathers of a peacock's neck. Shy and ill at ease, he bent so that we could not see his face. I looked up at you and threw open my hands in an angry and silent query, but you did not even turn your head. "You are beautiful, Prince," you said quietly to Lleu; "beautiful. I have never seen anyone so darkly beautiful."

"Go away," Lleu whispered without looking up. "Let me be. Why do you want to hurt me?"

"Dancer, swordsman," you said. "Black hair and eyes so deep, so dark: prince of Britain, first and foremost in the high king's sight. Are you not in every way my opponent? But for you, my son should have been heir to the high kingship."

"Godmother, must you?" I interrupted in disgust.

Lleu said irritably, "Medraut doesn't want the high kingship."

"I thought you might guess whom I meant," you said smoothly. "Have you ever asked him?"

Lleu rubbed his wrist and said irrelevantly, "I hate these peacocks."

"And me?" You smiled your incomplete smile.

He could not look at you directly. "I didn't think I did," he said. "But you seem to hate me."

"Of course not, ridiculous child," you answered. "Come, I will walk with you up to the villa." You offered a supporting arm to him, and he took it as though in a bewildered dream. "I shall tell the king," he said desperately.

"What shall you tell him?" you said. "You have nothing to tell him, Bright One." You turned his wrist over and ran your fingertips across the scratch you had given him. "Shall I salve this for you?"

"Oh, don't touch it," Lleu said. He pulled away from you and almost ran inside, stumbling a little. I scrambled to my feet and started to follow, but you caught my sleeve and held me back. "I said to stay," you repeated. "The little sun prince can survive a while without your protecting hand over his head."

I said sharply, "Indeed, why did you hurt him?"

"He neglected my child cruelly. I am only trying to punish him a little."

"It was a game. He has asked forgiveness and been forgiven. Why must you go on and on?"

"You thwart me, Medraut," you said quietly. The caged birds chattered and fluted over our heads. "You turn my threats aside."

I said through my teeth, "Godmother, I am struggling to keep peace in this house, and I hope you do feel thwarted."

You laughed again, and did not answer.

I found Lleu later, asleep on one of the wide windowsills in the still sunshine of the atrium, curled with his head cushioned on his hand and one of the cats dozing in the bend of his knee. Lleu asleep: and we had not been in the fields a full day. I bent to wake him, asking, "Nothing's wrong?"

He sat up stiffly, and the cat leaped away. "There couldn't be," he said. "I haven't eaten our own food in four days."

"But you're still so tired." I sat next to him on the stone sill.

"I think it is Morgause. I think her very touch must be poisonous," Lleu said, angry and weary, rubbing his wrist. "Could one do that?"

I smiled. "In hunting some people do use poisoned darts

90

or spears. But a touch will not suffice; the skin must be broken."

My words caught in my throat, and for a still moment Lleu and I looked at each other in a kind of mute horror. Then Lleu slowly turned his wrist over and held it before me. Shadows cast by the dull lead traceries of the window and light from the stippled, glinting glass panes mottled and slashed his bare arm. The narrow scrape there was barely deep enough to have bled, but the skin around it was red and hot to touch. I took Lleu's hand and held the scratch to my lips. "It smells of lavender," he said. "That wouldn't put me to sleep."

"No, it wouldn't." It smelled of aconite. The lavender did not hide it.

Lleu rubbed his eyes, and murmured, "I am very tired of this."

"I too." I snorted a little, wanting to sneer. Poisoned nails! You are exquisite, Godmother.

It was too late to go back to the fields, and there was no way for us to avoid eating supper with the rest of the family. We had scarcely been seated before you turned your slate-cold gaze on Lleu as he lifted his cup to drink. I leaped forward to knock his hand aside, and sent his cup flying across the atrium to smash against the windowsill in a storm of earthenware and cider.

Artos started up and struck the table with a blow that rattled the dishes. He thundered, "What the devil is the matter with you, Medraut?"

No answer came to mind. I stood before Artos without any excuse for my conduct.

91

"Medraut must think the cider's bad," Goewin said suddenly, breaking the awkward silence. "One of the bottles was off this morning."

"That's not true," I protested weakly.

"I tried it myself," Goewin insisted with careful and precise deliberation, looking directly at me as she spoke. "Though I may have been mistaken. Why take the chance?"

I clenched my hands to keep them from shaking. It was as close as I had ever come to lying. Ginevra said gently, "You'd better clear away the mess, Medraut."

Naked to the waist after a day at the gleaning, I climbed 'mong the red stones of the Edge far above field, village, and estate. I came upon Lleu drinking and washing his hands in the Holy Well, the shadowed stone trough high among the trees and rocks. The water was so dark I could not see his hands in it. "Need you come this far to drink?" I asked, and he answered me, "I think our well is poisoned." He drew his hands out of the spring, but the water that dripped from them was deep red, not clear. "You're bleeding!" I said, but he did not seem to hear. I made him turn around to face me, and his skin was white: not pale, but a dead, unreal white, like quartz or the moon. When I reached to take his hands his touch was cold and lifeless as stone. "You're dying," I whispered, and as I spoke he crumpled slowly to the ground.

Someone spoke my name in a low and urgent voice. I did not turn around, though I knew you stood behind me. "Medraut," I heard again, and a touch on my bare shoulder. I shook you off. "Godmother, no," I whimpered. My name again. Your touch.

Then a streak of pain fierce across my shoulder, as though I had burst into flame.

I cried out, "Curse you, lady!" and found myself in bed in my own room in the villa, risen on an elbow with one hand pressed to my shoulder. A dream. Only a dream. But the burning pain—

"Medraut, it's me," Goewin said. "Goewin. Goewin—not who you think."

I stared, only half-awake. Goewin stood a few steps away from me; when I woke she had shrunk back, startled. The little earthen lamp she held quivered in her hands, and lamp oil, cool now, was smeared across my shoulder. I thought she had burned me on purpose, to waken me. "You grow ruthless at last," I breathed. "I had not thought I must answer to two sphinxes: there is only supposed to be one."

Goewin asked unsteadily, "What is a sphinx?"

"A teller of riddles," I murmured as I examined the burn, "with a lion's body and a woman's head. She devours young men."

"I'm sorry," Goewin pleaded, a guilty Psyche unsure of what she had awakened. She knelt by my cot and said in a low and fervent voice, "You were sleeping curled with your back against the wall and your fists in knots, so deep in a dream I could not wake you. Ai, Medraut, you sleep as though you are in pain! I moved too quickly, and the lamp spilled, but it was an accident. I would never hurt you, never."

"Pass me the robe hanging over the chair," I said. She handed it to me, and looked away as I put it on.

"Is the burn all right?" she asked.

"Don't apologize again," I said, almost amused at her distress. I stood up and went to the open window to press my shoulder against the cold and soothing stone. The night outside smelled cool. Goewin stood behind me in the dark, trying to hold her little lamp steady. "What did you come here for?" I asked.

"Lleu is poisoned again," she said. "He woke me on his knees by my bed in such agony as I have never seen him. I could not make him get up. He thinks he is on fire."

I turned to face her. "How? What does he mean?"

"His mouth, his eyes, he says they burn. All inside him—"

"It will be spurge," I said. "I need milk. And get a better light." Automatically I began to ransack my shelves for an appropriate antidote, though I am ill supplied against anything so sinister and incomprehensible as your mind working in idleness and anger.

Lleu was in Goewin's chamber, crumpled on the floor next to her bed just as she had left him. He clung to the tapestry that hung there as though he were trying to support his weight against it. I had to pry the woolen folds from his fingers. When I forced him to let go he clutched at my own hands with the iron grip of desperation, and I could hardly shake him off long enough to set down the armful of bottles that I carried. I finally had to tie his hands. Then he managed to gasp in protest, "Oh: *no*." It seemed unspeakable that he should be made to endure such anguish, whatever the crime.

When the worst of the night was over Lleu cried out softly, "What is happening to me? I am being used as a pawn, a plaything—"

"How could it have happened?" Goewin said. "You had nothing to drink at supper."

"I had water afterward," Lleu said. "I may not have watched my cup closely enough."

"Surely you could taste spurge in water?" I said in wonder. "Ah, never mind. You'd already been bemused by aconite. Can you sleep now, little one?"

"I will try," Lleu said.

"Then good night," I said, gathering the vials littering the floor. "I will tell your father tomorrow. This—this is beyond my control."

I saw Lleu to his room, then went back to my own and scattered the debris of bottles and herbs in a disordered pile on my desk. The night was half gone. I was supposed to be at the copper mines just after sunrise, but I was determined I should speak to Artos before the day began. Sleep held only the promise of another nightmare. Instead of going back to bed I sat in the corridor before the door to my father's chambers, to be there when he woke. The stone floor was cold, the door hard against my back; the little burn on my shoulder had blistered so that now it stung and smarted. I drew my knees up against my chest and imagined I could watch there until morning.

Another dream.

I am alone in an abandoned garden. The stone walks are cracked and decaying; sweet flowering vines trail among the ruined roses, verdant beneath a sky of distant sapphire. But beyond the garden walls the land stretches cracked and desolate, sere earth and red rock. An arid river courses down the slope below the garden. I am in the south of Egypt, I think; If I follow the riverbed, I will find the Blue Nile and the high slopes and thin, clear air of Aksum. There is a figure sitting cross-legged on the bank of the dry river, the desert at his back, and I am surprised that in this land of dark-skinned people he is almost fair as I. When I approach to ask my way I find it is my brother. "This is not Africa," he tells me. "Do you not recognize the Mercian plain?"

And it is so. I can make out Shining Ridge and the Edge, though the forest is gone. "Where are the trees?" I ask.

He does not answer. He is bleeding again, as in the first dream, but this time from a wound in his side. Then it is not Lleu son of Artos, the prince of Britain, but Lleu Llaw Gyffes his namesake, the Bright One of the Steady Hand. Maimed and betrayed and enchanted, his hands become talons and his eyes grow round and gold: he is suddenly an eagle circling above my head and screaming.

It was Goewin screaming, and I was awake, huddled on the cold floor of the corridor. Artos stood in the doorway of his apartment, and Ginevra slipped past us with a lighted candle. I stood up quickly. "What in heaven's name is going on?" Artos demanded. Through the open door of Goewin's chamber we could hear Ginevra speaking in low tones of reassurement, and Goewin answering with shaking, muffled sobs. "What's wrong?" Artos called.

"A bad dream," Ginevra answered. "She is all right."

Artos turned to me. "My brave Goewin wakes screaming from nightmares," he said evenly and quietly. "Lleu can barely stay awake for two hours together, and I find you lurking outside my door in the middle of the night."

He paused, seeming to expect an answer, and I said uncertainly, "I must speak with you."

"If you were going to wait till morning you might have found the waiting easier in your chamber than in the corridor."

I looked down in apology.

"We can speak now," Artos said.

We went into his study. Artos sat at his desk and I lit the fire, glad to have some reason to occupy my taut hands, and glad of the extra time to think of how I must tell my story. "You haven't been sleeping well," Artos observed.

"No," I admitted.

"Sit down," he said.

"Thank you, sir." I sat, with my hands held carefully still on my knees; and then, without expression or bias, I told the king what you were doing to Lleu. Artos listened with equal reserve, without surprise, as though listening to a story about other people in another place and time.

"The simplest thing to do would be to send her away," I finished. "There need be no explanation, and there will be no scandal. No one in Camlan need know why she is leaving."

"Do you have proof of her treachery?" Artos said.

"Not beyond her own dark hint," I answered. "But someone is doing it, and it is like her. It is like something she once did to me." I spoke with difficulty, trying to be candid. "I grew to know her very well, the two years I stayed with her. She can be very cruel. I know there is no love between you, and I can't see that she has any reason to love your children."

"Has she reason to hate them?" Artos said quietly. "Well, it is true that she toys with people. When did this start?"

"I think it was the night Lleu fell asleep on the porch, and you had to carry him to bed," I answered. "It was raining."

Artos leaned forward, his hands clasped together on his desk, his expression still unbiased but his voice unforgiving. "That night you told me, when I asked you directly, that there was nothing wrong with Lleu," he said. "Were you lying then, or now, and to what end? And if you've been suspecting her of tormenting Lleu, why didn't you come to me at once?"

"I did not lie," I said. "I did not at first know what was happening, and I did not think he was in danger." Then I clenched my hands, except the fingers that do not bend, and spoke slowly and reluctantly. "Your sister: I am . . . I wanted to put an end to this before she invoked your wrath. She trusts me. At least—"

But before I could amend my words my father interrupted, "Then how can I?"

I began again. "I thought I could counter her myself. But Lleu is still being hurt. Knowing what she has done to me, what she might do to Lleu, makes me afraid of her."

"Medraut," said Artos quietly, "what has she done to you?"

I said nothing. I looked at my hands and carefully unclenched them, and did not answer.

"Well," said Artos mildly. "How am I to know what to guard against?"

"Before this summer you trusted me on my word alone. I can understand why that might change. But surely when I speak out against her, in defense of your son, you can't think that she has so great a hold over me?"

"I think that is precisely why you ask me to send her away," Artos answered. "Because she does. I think you're a deal more afraid of what she may do to you than of what she is doing to Lleu."

"That may be true." I sighed.

"Lleu is barely more than a child, and more dear to me than my own life," Artos said. "He still must be guarded from fear or pain. But I had thought you strong enough and wise enough to fend for yourself."

I sat still and silent. Does that mean, my father, that I can expect no protection or aid of you, that I must give and give of my loyalty and strength and never receive anything in return? No and no, I told myself; he could not mean that. I spoke at last, attempting calm and resignation. "But Lleu is in danger." I looked up at Artos, direct. "There's no sense in risking him only because you don't trust me."

"All right," Artos said. "We'll wake Morgause and you can accuse her openly."

"What, now?"

"Why not? Go wake her," Artos said. "If you would have me send her away, go wake her now, yourself, and bring her here."

I stared at him. *"Myself?"*

"Why not? She fostered you as her own child: you must have had cause to enter her private rooms before tonight."

He watched intently for my flinch, and saw it in hand, jaw, and eye. Furious at my transparency, I stood swiftly and said to my father, "Wait here." Taking a lamp from one of the wall brackets to light my way through the corridors, I considered Goewin's earlier accident and thought that I might pour the lamp's entire contents over your head to rouse you; but instead I sent in one of your handmaidens with a message that you were to meet your brother in the atrium. That was a petty cruelty, as it sounded like an invitation to a secret and midnight tryst. I woke and summoned the rest of the family as well, then returned to Artos. I bowed slightly to the high king and said, "Your family waits you in the atrium."

They were all there: Ginevra with Goewin's hand in hers, Goewin's stern face tearstained and dream haunted; Lleu, white with exhaustion and apprehension; all four of your children, who had been sleeping in the villa rather than one of the Halls, that they might be near you so long as you were in Camlan; and you, serene and regal in their midst. Artos surveyed his children and nephews, wife and sister, all waiting for him in the dim light of the brazier. "You wanted to speak to me, my lord?" you asked.

Artos sat down. "Medraut believes you are poisoning the prince of Britain," he said coldly.

"Such an accusation!" you answered calmly. Gareth squirmed a little in dismay, miserably biting his lips. Agravain stared at Lleu through narrowed eyes, as though his cousin were responsible. But none of them dared break his respectful silence. Lleu shivered, unable to meet your gaze, hating to be the focus of such malice.

"Such an accusation," you repeated, as though you enjoyed hearing yourself say so. "What proof do you have, Medraut? I have given no one any reason to believe evil of me."

Artos made an ironic gesture toward me and said dryly, "He stands before you, and you say that? Is he not reason enough?"

I turned to my father as though I had been struck. "I!"

He spoke in spiteful anger. Surely he said that without thinking; surely he did not believe it. I held my ground. "We were talking of the prince, not of me," I said to you. "Three times this week he's asked my aid to counter some foul drug that you slipped him in secret. When you used me this way I

100

said nothing and no one ever knew; but over the prince you have no such power, and I will not keep still."

"Loyal, so loyal," you sneered. Even Agravain shuddered. Lleu and Goewin had never seen you angry.

"It is not a question of loyalty," I answered. "I won't watch children being tortured. I won't watch you pretending to murder the high king's heir."

"Why not?" you said. "His murder would certainly be to your benefit."

"Mother!" Gwalchmei and Agravain exploded.

Artos said only, "Lleu, come here." Lleu moved to sit at his father's feet, and Artos firmly clasped one of the slim, shaking hands in his own. I stood straight and unmoving until the others were quiet again, then went on speaking to you. "But you haven't murdered him. You're tormenting him. Perhaps you do it to test my skill at remedies and antidotes. But I use my skill to serve the prince, not to answer to you."

"Your skill needs no test," you said. "I taught you well. As for answering to me, you will do whatever I demand of you." You were cold as I. "This trivial display of devotion to Artos and his little prince does not subordinate your bond to me." No one spoke. You demanded sharply, "Does it?"

It was hours past midnight. The rest of the household slept. Into the deep unbroken silence that followed your final question I barely managed to whisper the words, "My lord King, finish with her." I drew a deep breath and pressed my hand to my shoulder, regretting that I had neglected the burn there. So I stood, uncomforted, alone.

"You will leave in the morning," Artos said to you at last;

"and the boys will stay with me. They were to stay in any case. I will not let my nephews' minds be twisted by your treachery."

Gareth suddenly burst out with fretful sorrow, "Oh, Mother, how could you?" Devoted to you as they are, none of your sons expressed any doubt as to your guilt.

Agravain muttered fiercely, "I'd count it lucky should you pay such notice to any of us."

This you ignored, and asked of Artos, "Have I leave to travel south to visit our mother—yours and mine—before I return to the Islands?"

Agravain snapped, "Anyone fool enough to talk to the high king like that—after practicing witchery on his heir—"

"Agravain," you said gently.

He looked away. "Excuse me, Mother," he murmured bitterly.

"No need, Agravain," Artos said. "Yes, you may visit Igraine. I will even provide you with an escort. They will be ready to leave as soon as you have gathered clothes for the journey. Your menagerie, the rest of your belongings, and your servants will be sent after you. No one will be told of this meeting, but you will leave tomorrow."

"The menagerie is my gift to you."

Artos sighed. "Spare me, Morgause. Your gifts to Lleu have been sufficient."

"Is that all?" you said.

"There is more I could say," Artos answered evenly, "but none of it is necessary."

Lleu lifted his head impulsively to look at his father, and at the sudden movement you turned on him. "Prince of Britain," you said with real hatred, "indeed. You are so young, so frail! Hardly more than a rare ornament, a plaything, to be used and discarded at leisure."

"Lleu's no more frail than any of your own boys," Artos said tersely. "As to playthings, you seem to find more amusement in your collection of peacocks than in your husband's children."

"And truly your other son is more useful to me," you replied, glancing at me. Agravain stared with narrowed eyes, envious, desperate for your favor. All your children are.

"Medraut fought honestly enough against you to prevent Lleu from being hurt," Goewin cried. Her loyalty shamed me.

"No need, Goewin," said Artos, as he had to Agravain. "I have finished. All of you: enough snarling at one another."

You bowed deeply to Artos and kissed his hand. "Then I will take my leave of you and prepare for my journey. I thank you for your lenience, my lord." You turned to Lleu and knelt before him. "And you, little lord," you said softly, holding out your hands, "have I your pardon?"

He glared at you and answered vehemently, "No. You don't have my pardon. And I think you can guess why I would rather not take your hands."

"You know I would not have slain you in your father's house," you said.

"I know," he replied. "You might not understand: it was knowing you did not mean to slay me that frightened me most."

You answered with a full smile, glowing and warm in the dim light. "I do understand," you said. "That was my intention."

At dawn I fled to the mines, and stayed almost till sundown. You were gone when I returned. The household was still unsettled; your servants huddled together in whispering pairs or else were busy packing your belongings. I could not face your children, though it meant little to them whether or not I met their eyes. I sought solace in the young bats, and Goewin found me there, standing under the eaves outside my chamber. When she came close I opened my cupped hands, and the bat I held blinked sleepily at her in the failing daylight. She touched its silken back gently. "They trust you now," she said, "even the grown ones."

"It is very peculiar," I answered quickly, "because no one—" I stopped, and glanced at her to smile apologetically. "They are beautiful, aren't they?"

She gazed at me and said, "You seem so tired."

"I am tired."

"You could have easily let Lleu die, or even arranged his death yourself, this last week. Your hands are so strong you could crush that delicate creature you hold, but you do not hurt it." She sighed. "Medraut, do you ever dream of anything but your mother?"

I opened my hands and raised them sharply, and the bat took wing into the lavender darkness. I did not look at Goewin. "How much I have betrayed to you in one way or another," I said bleakly.

"Do you?" she pressed.

"I had not dreamed of her in over a year," I answered in a low voice, "and this summer I have dreamed of almost nothing else." But I managed to smile at her. "Tonight I intend to dream of snow on the high moors."

IX
The Copper Mines

I tried, I tried. But my fortune, with the summer, was at its ebb. To see you again, to part from you again, made me feel I was an unwelcome shadow of yourself lurking at the edges of other people's lives. Your children seemed to settle easily into their new home, never thinking to connect themselves or me to your disgrace. But I could find no simple way, no quick way back to the even tranquillity of the previous year. When I returned to my room the first night after you had gone, the very disorder of the shelves that hung there seemed to reflect my mood. Beneath scattered bottles the plans for the blocked mine shaft lay unfinished on my desk, and now I found them to be flawed and ridiculous. Heedless of waste, I burned the offending scraps of parchment and threw out the empty vials.

I dreamed of Aksum again and started awake in the dead of night with the obvious solution to the unyielding cave wall. Kidane had once taken me to see the mine where he bought gold; there they had broken the rock in the pits with fire and vinegar, as the Romans had done, shoring the tunnels with arches of stone. I told Cado of this. He teased me for being high-minded, foreign, and old-fashioned, but behind all that he was intrigued with the idea. I knew a little of how it was done, and now Cado and I learned to split stone with fire. We worked together in the open air during moments of leisure. We blistered and burned our hands like children playing a forbidden game, intoxicated with the success of our experiments. One failed attempt made us laugh so drunkenly that neither of us could hold the flint steady to light another flame.

But our growing expertise sobered us, and at last we requested permission from Cadarn to fire the wall of our shaft. We were far enough from the chief mine workings that we would cause no danger beyond our own tunnel. Together with the six men under our leadership we shored our corridor with beams of oak, and began to break down the wall. We worked with slow but visible success; in a week we moved perhaps three feet forward in the tunnel. We came at last to a narrow cleft that bore promise of a cavern beyond, and the walls were streaked thickly with the green and blue of copper ore. After the last spirit-soaked rags had been forced into the dark fault and lit, and after the choking smoke had cleared, we found we had forced a passage wide enough for a man to slip through.

Cado went first, a lantern in his hand. He squeezed through the gap and then seemed to halt just beyond our reach and view, curiously silent and still. "What is it?" I called to him. "Are we through?"

He did not answer at once. When he spoke his voice was firm and low: "Come see, Medraut. The way's narrow, but I think you can get by."

It was narrow indeed; Tegfan, who is short but broad-chested, could not follow. But the others came behind me, curious and anxious to witness the proof of our success.

Such proof: utterly unexpected, and weirdly beautiful. The passage we had forced opened not to a cavern or tunnel but to a little natural chamber, with a low ceiling and rounded walls. The walls were infused with thick green streaks of malachite and smooth red clay, almost evenly spaced between fields of pale limestone: and sweeping across the curve of the walls were pictures like nothing I have seen before or since, painted by some human hand countless ages past. The images were of a tall, broad, heavy-antlered deer that dwarfed the awkward figures who appeared to stalk it. Here at the hill's heart, this strange and savage hunt endured in the darkness of a forgotten time.

"But how did it get here?" I wondered aloud.

"There used to be another passage in," Cado said, holding up his lantern. "See! The clay's filled the entrance, not even a gap in the seam. How old can this be!"

I said with conviction, "I must show Lleu."

"Who patches tile pictures with such love and skill." Cado laughed. "Send Tegfan to get him. We'll set up the supports till they get back."

So it was that within the hour Lleu stood with me and Cado and our workmen in the hidden place under the earth, dark eyes ablaze with torchlight and excitement. He laughed aloud in the sheer pleasure of sharing in this secret beauty; laughed with real joy, though I know he was afraid to be so far from air and light and the open spaces of day. He lingered over each painting, forcing himself to wrench his gaze from one to the next. "This artistry, in such a place!" he exulted. "I couldn't have dreamed such a thing if I hadn't seen it."

But beneath our talk and laughter there came the ominous sound of a cataract of falling pebbles. They skittered down the curved wall across the flank of the painted deer, and came to rest at Cado's feet. Tegfan called from the other side of the passage, "Should we go up until the ground settles?"

I looked with question at Cado, and he nodded. Into our sudden stillness a larger eddy of earth trickled down the rock wall. "Take the prince outside," Cado said calmly.

More slender than any of us, Lleu slid through the narrow passage with barely an effort. I went after him, and called back to the others in a low voice, "Follow at once, as close as you can." I picked up a lantern and put a hand on Lleu's shoulder to guide him forward; and the ceiling closed in behind us.

Tegfan croaked, "Go," and the three of us ran up the tunnel. We could hear, could always hear at our back the inner groaning of the disturbed hillside. Stones fallen from the ceiling struck at our heels. We were halfway to the outer cavern when the floor itself buckled, and Tegfan fell. I turned to give a hand to him, and shouted at Lleu, "Go on!" But there was no time. "Shield your head!" I cried then, and struck Lleu between the shoulders with such force that he was shoved stumbling perhaps ten steps farther up the tunnel. Off-balance, I too fell sprawling forward; the lantern hit the floor and flickered out. Then I could find neither strength nor courage to pick myself up as the ceiling fell in about my ears, and I did not dare to stir until the rumbling and crashing stopped.

When all I could hear was my own uneven breath, I moved to get up, but a fallen beam held me pinned to the floor by one foot and the opposite wrist. I moved my free arm a scant few inches and found, by chance, the lantern. Lleu's voice came unsteadily out of the dark: "Medraut?"

I answered quietly, "Lleu? I still have the lantern: Come light it."

I stretched my arm to him; he found me and clutched at my hand. He was on his knees, crawling, afraid to stand. He whispered, "Your hands are like ice."

"Light the lantern," I returned.

He did, revealing what was left of the shaft. Behind me, where the debris went deeper, Tegfan lay senseless, buried up to his waist. Behind us both, the fallen earth and rock sloped upward to the tunnel's roof to fill the shaft beyond. There was no sign of Cado or the five others who had been with him.

"You're not hurt?" I said to Lleu. He shook his head. The lantern quaked in his hand, so he set it on the floor.

I stretched my free arm toward Tegfan, but could not reach him. "See if—," I said to Lleu, then barked out, *"No!"* as he began to climb the pile of debris to reach Tegfan. "Distribute your weight. Lie down and stretch up the slope." He obeyed numbly, and felt for the pulse in one of Tegfan's limp wrists. "Don't use your thumb," I directed.

Lleu said at last, "He's all right."

"Hold the lantern up there: can you see any sign of the rest?"

"There's nothing, sir," Lleu whispered.

"Help me." I could not sit up, trapped as I was; propped awkwardly on an elbow, almost flat on my back, I struggled to shift the beam that held me prisoner. But even when Lleu pulled with me we could not move it. "Take the lantern," I said quietly, "and go for help. Don't run; we may not have much air. If there is another tremor, don't come back. Did you mark the way out?"

He nodded. "But sir—," he began. "Are you hurt?"

I shook my head. "But Tegfan must be. And the rest of us, Cado—" I bit the words off, scarcely able to speak aloud what I was thinking. *"Six men!"* I gasped, incredulous. *"Six men,* and I responsible!"

Lleu bent, impulsively, to drop a quick kiss on my forehead before he took the lantern and started up the tunnel. I watched him go, the light with him growing more distant. When he turned the corner there was only a faint bloom of yellow warmth against the far wall: and after that nothing but blackness, and I alone.

I can hardly bear to tell of this.

I thought I must go mad waiting there for very long. But soon, soon, four men from the upper shafts came down with lanterns and shovels. Tegfan—he was senseless through all our cautious work to free him, and I started to splint his legs as best I could before we carried him out. But the roof began to tremble again. We abandoned the tools, for it took all four men from the upper shafts to carry Tegfan. The tunnel shuddered and rattled as we half ran, half crawled upward, dodging showers of clay and dust. It was agony to put weight on the foot that had been trapped; I dragged myself behind the others, frantic lest I should cause their destruction as well.

The ground and ceiling beyond the cut doorway to the

main tunnel were steady, and a little crowd stood waiting for us there. They had not dared to venture beyond the stone lintels and oak beams that supported the entrance, and sent up a sober cheer of thanks as we burst gasping into their midst. I stood just beyond the tremorous shaft, shaking so that I could not hold the horn of ale someone offered me. One said, "My lord, can you see to Tegfan's legs?" Another asked, "Will we be able to search for the others that were with you?"

For answer—it was an answer—came a low rumble and clatter from deep in the tunnel, and the lower shaft collapsed. It sealed itself from the roots outward, as though some starved inner core hungered to consume the entire hillside. I have killed another friend, I thought, buried alive six men; and so imagined the abyss closing around me, and plunged into the devouring darkness.

Light mist on my face, then, and wind. I opened my eyes to a gray sky that seemed blindingly bright. I lay on the flat ground just beyond the quarry, with Caius and Cadarn kneeling by me. "Lleu," I gasped, and sat up too fast. The red stone tilted about me. "Where is Lleu?"

"Home," Caius said. "Unhurt, not so much as a scratch. Gently, lad." He helped me to sit up. "Gods, what a day for you. Can you walk?"

I hesitated to answer. Cadarn said, frowning, "Let me see your foot."

It was already so swollen that I could not get my boot off. "We're shutting down for the day," Cadarn said. "The king has sent Caius to see you home. You can borrow one of the ponies if you can't walk."

I could not even take the reins, for my wrist was also badly bruised. When we reached the villa Caius helped me to my room and sent for Aquila; they had to cut away my boot before Aquila could bind my ankle. Lleu brought me supper, and with it the message that Artos wanted to speak to me when I had finished. I could not eat. I said that I would go at once to Artos, and Lleu soberly offered me his shoulder for support. Outside his father's study he said to me, with apology and pity in his voice, "I am to be present at this interview."

Artos was pacing, waiting for us. "Get Medraut a chair," he said curtly for greeting. Now he stood still, to lean against his desk and face me. "Do you know what angers me most in this miserable day's work?" he demanded.

I shook my head. I could not look at him. "Tell me."

"That Lleu was there when it happened. That you knew the chance you took with the explosives: you even thought to get Cadarn's permission before you used them. That you knew the shaft might not hold up, and yet you had Lleu down there with you not so much as an hour after you had broken through the wall. Trust! My God, Medraut, what would you have me think of you? What kind of an idiot would take his sovereign's heir down a forced mining tunnel before the earth even had a chance to settle?"

"He is not hurt," I whispered.

"And for that you'd do well to offer up a fervent prayer of thanks," Artos snapped. "And meantime pray as well for those men under your command, who also trusted you, Iaen and Gwyn, Cynedyr, Cado——"

"*I know their names!*"

Artos hit me, hard, in cold fury.

"Father!" Lleu cried out softly.

Artos turned on him. "Not a word from you, my Bright One. You've been little wiser than your brother, today." He faced me again, and spoke more gently. "Only I expect more of you, Medraut."

"I spoke without thinking," I said in a low voice. "But Cado was my friend. Forgive me, sir."

"And forgive me also, Medraut." Artos sighed. He shook his head and leaned against the desk again, folding his arms and regarding me with sorrow and anger. "I have never lost so many lives at once unless it was in a battle."

I shook with pent despair. "An accident—I could not stop it happening—"

"I know." He spoke evenly now, in control of his anger. "But the fact remains that Lleu was with you when it happened." Lleu sighed this time, but held silent. Artos continued, "Your transgression is in a lack of responsibility, Medraut, and as punishment I can only see fit to deny you that responsibility in the future. You are stripped of your foremanship. You may not return to work in the copper mines until Tegfan's legs are healed. You will remain within the villa for the rest of the week, and for a month after that you will not leave the grounds of the estate unescorted."

I bowed my head. Behind me, I heard Lleu say, "And I?"

Artos answered gently, "I think such an experience has been punishment enough for you."

I looked up sharply at my father, and challenged: "Is Lleu not old enough to choose where he will or will not go? Is he never to be given any responsibility, not even for himself? Can you ensure that he never kills anyone by accident, any more than you can protect him from being struck by lightning?" I stopped for breath, my heart racing. Words came to

113

me out of the dark, out of memory: *"'Am I my brother's keeper?'"*

Artos did not move. He said in deadly quiet: "You will return to your room."

The following week was the blackest period of my life. I could not walk for several days, and I had sufficient leisure to imagine a half dozen ways I might have avoided so great a disaster; I sat at my desk for hours with my face in my hands and could think of nothing else. Artos allowed me to join the sad and bleak little funeral service held at the mines. But most of the week I was confined to my room, alone.

As I began to accept that for all its horror the ordeal was over, and irreversible, I tried to think of other things. I distilled oils for Ginevra, exotic but harmless essences such as cinnamon and vanilla; and I read. I read over again almost all the books I own, and some others I found in my father's study, abandoning myself especially to those that are not true: Irish legends, Roman poetry, the few Greek plays that I have in Latin translation. One evening in November Artos discovered me over one of these, weeping in still and stricken silence. At first I did not even notice he was there, standing behind me, until he laid a heavy hand on my shoulder. Startled, I could only stare at him in inarticulate shame that he should find me in tears over a fiction.

But he read aloud over my shoulder, "'I weep for you as well, though I can't see you, imagining your bitter life to come.'"

I turned the pages over and wiped my eyes. "I beg your pardon, sir."

"I also have shed tears for the king of Thebes," Artos

said. "My marksman: I have a task for you that I think you will enjoy."

I could feel my hands tensing with relief. I was wretched with the enforced idleness of the last month.

Artos said, "I want you to teach Lleu to hunt."

We took five hounds and rode south. The Mercian plain was at this time of year gray and brown, with clouds resting and tearing on the distant peaks that rimmed the horizon. There had been one or two light, insignificant snowfalls, and patches of snow lay unmelted here and there beneath the trees. The lake where the fisheries are was covered with a thin scale of ice, and our horses' hooves sent a few pebbles skidding across the barely solid sheet as we rode by. The gravel made a surprisingly loud noise as it hit the ice, echoing and squealing like metal on stone. Lleu, who had scarcely spoken to me since our session with Artos, started at the unearthly sound like a nervous cat.

"You've nothing to fear, Bright One," I said lightly. "I'm not going to touch my bow today."

"You're not shooting at all?"

"No. You are."

I thought: You are going to kill, my brother; you are going to take the life of another living being, and forever you will be accountable for that life. As I am for many lives lost, animal and man.

I added aloud, "For after all, it's no little thing to feed yourself, my lord Prince."

Lleu threw me a resentful look and did not answer. He knew the purpose of our hunting together.

Before long we came upon a stag, full-grown but young.

We could not get close to it at first, and soon we had lost both deer and hounds. We slowed our pace and halted. I sounded a long horn call and we heard the far-off yell of the dogs in answer, but Lleu made no move to follow. "Do you come?" I said impatiently. "Give chase!"

I reached out and pulled at his reins, then tore after him as his horse started suddenly away. We rode through a tangle of dripping trees, then burst into a cloudy brown clearing, silvered over with mist, to see the rusty deer bright bounding through the winter bracken. "Your bow!" I cried. "Now!"

Lleu obediently sent an arrow streaking just between the graceful antlers, harmless.

I pulled alongside him and reached out to snatch his reins again, bringing him abruptly to a halt. "You do it on purpose," I hissed. "That is the trouble, is it not? In practice you can hit a moving target at twice that distance. I told your father I would teach you to hunt, and if we must spend the rest of the night riding you are not returning to be petted and praised by the high king till you have killed. You have the skill." Lleu's face was ashen. I added with cool menace, "I swear by the Wild Hunt if you do not bring down that stag at the next opportunity, I will make you eat its entrails when you do." The deer and dogs had already disappeared into the trees at the opposite side of the clearing. I struck Lleu lightly across the face with his own reins. "Now, follow!"

He tore away from me, riding blindly and furiously. I caught up with him among the trees, and we rode together in silence except for the horses' hooves thundering hollow on damp turf. Ahead of us, the young buck was tiring visibly. "Now, Bright One," I said. "Strike."

Lleu bent his bow with reluctant hands. Despite his hesitation he took the creature with an arrow in its throat.

"Ha!" I drew my horse to a halt. "Beautiful!"

But he had not killed it. The lean, quick hounds leaped for it like gray flames. "No!" Lleu cried. He slid from his horse and threw himself among the dogs, snatching at the collar of his own. "Here, sir! Back!" Clinging to his straining hound, he shouted wrathfully, "Call off your horrible dogs!"

I called the dogs and dismounted. "Better that you finish than that they do," I said, and gave Lleu my hunting knife.

"Oh, I can't!" he gasped. He knelt next to the fallen deer with one hand lightly resting on a short, proud antler, and his hound and Goewin's whining at his shoulders.

"Would you have it die slowly, then?" I said.

He held on to the antler and moved the heavy head to stretch out the animal's throat; its steaming breath was strangled and uneven. I began to say, "If you don't—"

But he drove the blade to cut deep across the stag's throat. And just as he looked up at me, another deer came through the trees toward us: not chased and so not running, a dark doe, almost black. Goewin's hound darted after it.

"Take her, Prince!"

Lleu stood up and shot, elegantly and miserably. I laughed. "It's true; you could have hit every animal you've ever aimed at. What a strange little idiot you are." I glanced at his gray, bleak face and said in a gentler voice, "Give me the knife, I'll help you. If you are to be high king you will have to kill more than deer, eventually."

"I know," he said.

"There is some balance to all things, Lleu. The stag's

death gives us winter meat; and the power to kill, or to heal or to judge, carries with it a great weight of responsibility."

"I know." Lleu pushed his hair back from his forehead wearily. "I know. You are teaching me. Only don't expect me to thank you for this lesson."

"You never do," I said, thinking of another beautiful stag, and the huntsmen buried beneath the hill.

X

Revelation

Tegfan's legs healed slowly. At the end of the year he still could not walk. Though by now I was no longer confined to the estate and could come and go as I pleased, I was still idle; I was desperate to be given even the smallest of tasks. Close to Christmas, Caius sent me to the smithy with a mare that was to be shod. While Gofan worked over the new shoes, Marcus said to me casually, "Will you be rhyming with us this year, lord?"

"How do you know I ever did?" I asked. It had been eight years since my last rhymers' pageant, the ritual Midwinter's mumming at Elder Field. There had been no revelry the year of the famine, and that sobriety had also tainted the following Christmas.

"Caius tells me that when you were a boy you took the part of the Old Year's son, the Winter Prince." Marcus grinned at me. "I, of course, have taken on that role in your absence, but you may try to wrest it from me if you like."

"No fear of that," I returned. "I think I am no longer suited to act the young hero. And I thought you'd stopped the play."

"We haven't done it since you've been back," Gofan said. "But this year . . . for the most part this has been a golden year. It bears celebrating."

"There is a conspiracy abroad to cast you as the Magician," Marcus added.

Magician—I? The rhymers' play is a pageant for midwinter, celebrating the return of the sun at the dark time of the year's closing. The Magician is the bringer of light, the figure whose task it is to recall the murdered harvest lord to life. I thought it bitter irony they should see me fit for such a role. But Marcus tossed my objections aside, and even Gofan laughed. They said I was the most skilled healer the villagers had ever known, and that I was missed in the mines and the fields. I warmed to their friendship and flattery. So I came to join the informal and haphazard rehearsals for the play; I was once again made welcome by the high king's friends and servants, at a time when I had a great need of laughter and companionship.

Christmas brought cold. The year's end was marked by clear, bitter nights on fire with white starlight. There was no snow, only the biting, bone-deep chill that froze the little rivers solid and kept the African cats curled together on the warm tiles of the atrium floor. But the granaries were full, and the storehouses crowded with dried fruit and salted meat. The people of Camlan and Elder Field wrapped themselves well with wool and fur and laughed at the hard frost, for they were busy with the preparation of a joyous Midwinter's feast. I was torn between full enjoyment of the celebration and my nagging, lingering burden of guilt for the tragedy I had caused in the early autumn. A Christmas of glitter and sweetness, which I thought myself unworthy to share in. And yet I could not help but share in it.

On Midwinter's Eve I returned to the villa after a long day spent on the threshing floor in one of the village barns, where we had been making rhymers' costumes out of straw and evergreen. All the family were at leisure in the atrium. Gareth sat in the window seat with one of the cats, while Gwalchmei played idly upon a small harp; Agravain, in an uncharacteristic fit of patience, was teaching Gaheris and Lleu an obscure dicing game. Goewin and her mother were arguing agreeably over a parchment spread on the table. I scooped up one of the cats and nuzzled it beneath my chin; its fur was the color of the dry savanna country of Aksum before the rains, warm. The cat shrank away from the chill of my skin, and I thought suddenly of Lleu when he was no more than five years old: allowed outside in winter for the first time in his life, laughing as he winced away from a handful of snow that I held against his cheek.

"It's still so cold out?" Artos inquired from his couch.

"Cruel," I said.

"Did you see Tegfan today?"

"I did. He says the pain has stopped. I don't want him walking yet, though."

"Wise, my marksman," Artos said. He stood before me to tease my cat beneath its chin. "I have said nothing, but I know what a trial this healing is for you. Your patience is to be admired."

His praise, only his simplest kind word, could kindle warmth in me. I said quietly, "Thank you, sir."

I put down the cat and began to take off my gloves. I had scarcely set them on the table before Caius came in and said to Artos, "There are pilgrims at the gate."

"Beggars?" Artos asked. "Who would be out on such a night?"

Caius pressed his lips together tightly. He spoke so that only Artos and I could hear him. "The boy who let them in says it is your sister."

"No," I said aloud. Artos glanced at me sharply. "You sent her back to the Orcades!" I protested.

Artos shook his head. "She pled illness earlier in the season and requested that I allow her to postpone the journey. She is supposed to stay in Ratae Coritanorum, south of here, until spring."

"But, sir!" I exclaimed in outrage. "You did not tell me!"

Artos looked at me with eyebrows raised. "I have made no secret of her plans," he said. "Her children are always clamoring for news of her." Then his face hardened, and he turned to Caius. "Though I did not expect her here. She tries my patience." He beckoned to Ginevra, and Caius explained the matter to her in low tones.

"I will not have her here," I hissed. "I will not live in fear of her."

"It is Christmas!" Artos returned. "What would you have me do, send her back into this cold?"

"She chose to come!"

Ginevra said, "We cannot send her away. But we can guard her. Artos, let her stay only until the weather breaks; and treat her as a prisoner. Her servants can sleep in the

Great Hall, and Aquila can search her belongings for any poisons. We will give her a single room to her own use, but she will be watched always, never left alone. Will that ease your mind, Medraut?"

"Guard her servants as well," I said hoarsely.

Artos nodded. "See to it, Caius."

"Shall I bring her in, then?" Caius asked, and Artos nodded again. Suddenly suffocating in the heat of the room and the fur and wool I wore, I said, "I'll go with you, Caius." For I knew I must face you, and any wrath you bore me from our last parting, and I did not want to wait.

The night was fearfully cold. Your party huddled shivering in the courtyard beneath two or three guttering torches. A servant girl held your gloved hands nestled between her own, and rubbed them fiercely and frantically; but you pushed her aside when you saw me, to clutch at my jacket and press yourself against my chest, silent and shaking. In apprehension I put up a hand to thrust you away, mistrusting you, but stopped in wonder as my fingers brushed the icy tears across your cheek.

"Godmother?"

Still you said nothing, so I let you cling to me and quench your silent tears against my shoulder. I had never known you to weep at anything, ever. I said softly, "Godmother, speak to me."

You raised your head and gazed at me with frightened eyes of darkling blue, the tear tracks glittering in the torchlight. "I did not think we could get this far. It is a week's journey from Ratae Coritanorum, but it was warm when we left—the weather turned around midweek. I would never have attempted to come if I had known it would turn so cold.

Oh, Medraut, Artos will not turn me away, will he? He must give me shelter tonight—I never meant to put myself at his mercy like this! I am so afraid—"

"You are not afraid of anything," I said with a laugh. Your gloved hands tightened into fists against my chest.

"No!" you whispered, and buried your face beneath my chin. I was so well wrapped against the chill that I could not even feel your breath; it was as though there were no warmth in you at all. You whispered into my scarf, "But I am afraid now. I—I am no longer young, and I have no authority to speak of, and I do not want to freeze to death tonight."

Then I saw that you clung to me for support as well as for comfort. I murmured, "You may stay, but Artos will treat you as a prisoner. Your things are to be searched, and you are to be guarded at all times. Will you submit to that?"

Your bent shoulders heaved as you wept soundlessly. "Yes. Damnation take my brother and his kingdom! Only let me be warm tonight."

I looked up at Caius, who watched you with eyes of contempt and of sympathy. "Take her in," he said. "I'll see to her servants."

Camlan spent the following day preparing for a shamelessly pagan festival. The Christian celebration was to be kept, more solemnly, on Christmas day, but now we fastened holly at the windows to ward off evil. The hearth in the center of the Great Hall was piled with faggots of slender birch logs bound with red ribbon and gold thread, and the villa was sweet with garlands of forced apple blossom. The day passed quickly, the shortest in the year. Once it was dark the household waited ready in restless excitement; the rhymers' pageant would begin the revelry, but first we must perform

"—son of our father and your mother, who are brother and sister," Lleu finished in the same hot, hollow voice.

"Our mother, his true mother?" Agravain said slowly. "But they two . . ." He gazed at me through narrowed eyes. Gareth stared silently at the floor in helpless embarrassment.

I held quiet. My limbs were of a sudden brittle as figured ivory. I whispered, "Need my parentage be discussed tonight?"

"As I am prince of Britain you dare not contest anything of which I wish to speak," Lleu said, and Goewin hit his elbow and said harshly, "*Stop this!* Haven't you said enough already?"

But I had regained my composure. I moved to kneel before Lleu on the floor, my head bowed; even when we both knelt I was still taller. I kissed my fingertips and held them to the golden band at Lleu's temples. "Your Highness. I most humbly beg your pardon." I raised my head to gaze at him for a long moment, until he could not bear it and must turn away. Then I got to my feet and left them.

Driven by fury, as though in a dream, I went to my chamber and changed to the magnificent robe Kidane had given me. It is of fine black woven wool, the upper sleeves and shoulders inlaid with intricate small panels of indigo Oriental silk. The sleeves were made to fit close, so that I could wear over them the rare, ancient warrior's bracelets from Cathay, the miniature dragons that coil heavily from wrist to elbow. They are a symbol of power; they are the mark of royalty. So Turunesh cautioned me when she gave them to me, and I had never worn them, afraid to wear them in idleness. In childish vanity I wore them now. But I could not keep Lleu's shameful derision from echoing in my memory; I spoke to the empty room through clenched teeth, and said aloud, "I am the high king's eldest son." The words were meaningless.

You sat well guarded in the single small room they had allowed to you. Unbidden I bent to your embrace. You drew me down with arms that for all their slender elegance seemed strong as wire, until I knelt at your side with my head cradled against the soft wool of your gown. Your touch was gentle as rain, but I was taut, quivering with anger and hatred—I could not speak or even weep, overwhelmed by such fury.

"Hush, my child," you said, and, "hush."

I knelt there long, so long. The strong, thin healer's hands that lifted and twisted my hair were achingly gentle, but that familiar touch had never truly afforded me solace or comfort. Even now you did not ask what had happened. When I made no move to raise my head you murmured, "Where did you get such bracelets? The high king himself wears nothing so splendid."

"They were given to me in Africa."

"Given?"

I raised my head at last. "Aye, given, Godmother."

"This Turunesh was more to you than merely your patron's daughter," you mused. "Why did you come back?"

"This is my home," I said bitterly.

"Medraut, look at me." You cupped my face in your hands. "You are the true prince of this land," you said softly. "If you could see yourself! Dangerous, yet of curious grace and beauty; such chaos in your eyes. If it were in my power you would be heir to all—"

"Ah, Godmother, don't," I sneered. "It has never been in your power."

"Nothing is, anymore. Artos will not even let me come to the Great Hall for the feast tonight." You rose and left me kneeling there and walked across the room to open a carven box and sift the contents through your fingers. "Let me bind back your hair, as I used to. I have some gold wire I can twist to make you a chaplet."

"No!" I spat. "I'll wear nothing that looks like a crown."

You turned to gaze down at me. A slow smile played about your lips, a mere twitch at the corner of your mouth. "So that is the way of it," you said softly, and from another casket drew out a strip of black silk. "This, then." You stood by me and banded the ribbon across my forehead. I rose and shook out the heavy folds of my robe; you stood away, admiring me as a craftsman admires the work of his hands. "You must have an eardrop as well." I let you fix one on me, a heavy jewel of gold and jet that I think I have worn before.

"'In the midst of the lampstands,'" you murmured low, "'one clothed with a long robe and with a golden girdle round his breast; his head and his hair were white as white wool, white as snow, his eyes were like a flame of fire.'"

I stared at you. "That is from Revelation."

"Had you been speaking of it?" you gasped in mock surprise, amusement in your gaze. "I know what happened. Agravain was here before you, asking terrible questions of me. But I have set his jealous heart at ease."

"How could you?"

"I lied to him," you answered casually, and commenced to brush your hair. "There's a riddle for you, my virtuous child:

129

Is it worse to deny the truth, or to hide it? I doubt you'll hurry to set him straight."

I did not know what to answer. As I hesitated, the guardswoman at the door entered; she said to me, "My lord, Caius is asking for you."

"Send him in," you told her.

"The rhyming!" I sighed. I had forgotten in my anger. "I cannot go dressed like this."

"Why not?" you answered. And Caius exclaimed as he came in, "Medraut, you look a prince!" He laughed, and came to stand before me and clasp my shoulders as he admired my finery. "You need not change. You know the costumes were made to fit over our clothes."

"Even so."

"No fear, we'll make it part of the performance. I'll get you a cloak. No one must see you yet."

"Medraut!"

I turned back to you before I left the room. You said quietly, "Come bid me good night when all is over."

We took the pageant from door to door throughout the village, nameless, anonymous luck-bringers in our shaggy and shapeless costumes. Our small party had become a parade when we arrived back at the estate, for many of the villagers had followed us on their way to the feast at Camlan. Warm with the cider and ale of Elder Field, we burst shouting into the crowd gathered in the Great Hall, who returned our shouts for greeting. Then Gofan in his great voice called out the opening lines of the pageant:

"Way! Make way!
Yield the floor, clear the way!

We'll mend all evil's ill with mirth
On this Midwinter's Day."

He commanded silence. The laughing crowd stood still.

"Under your green-girt beams we come
Neither to beg nor borrow;
Happy we play upon your hearth
To speed away all sorrow.
We are the season's rhymers!
Cry welcome to us here!
Fortune we bring to field and fold
At the closing of the year."

Now our audience was rapt. The words were old and familiar, and it was too long since they had been spoken in this hall. Caius stepped forward into the small circle of clear ground, the red, holly-trimmed hood hiding his face so that the white linen mask beneath could not even be glimpsed.

"In come I, the Old Year,
Keeper of this fruitful land.
Your stout hoards of grain, ale, and meat
Are blessed beneath my hand."

A ragged cheer went up. They were apt words from the steward of the estate, but no one was sure that it was Caius.

"Here is your hope, here is your bread,
Your shield against the dark's sharp blast:
Who boldly dares before me stand
To lay me low at last?"

Bedwyr answered him, the high king's swordsman, gray-hooded and glittering with icicles of silver foil and mica.

"In come I, the New Year;
The snow falls at my word.
The black months wheel around ere Spring,
Ice-edged as my cold sword.
I am the one stronger than all
Who march in this parade:
Which of these gay retainers, lord,
Dare turn aside my blade?"

Marcus, in his crown of forced flowers:

"In come I, the Winter Prince,
Son of the Year that's gone;
Green ivy, hawthorn, and holly I bear
For pledges of the returning Sun.
I will fight for the Old Year:
Though the grim Midwinter's rod
Strikes the soil, soon the young Sun
Will stir the Spring's triumphant sod."

Bedwyr as the New Year answered:

"Pull out your sword, young Harvest Lord,
Defender of the Sun
As the Year dies, so you shall fall—
You and the Old Year both I shall have
Before I quit this hall."

Gofan brought forth the swords, staves bound with ribbons and green leaves. Half serious, half in jest, Marcus and Bedwyr began the ritual duel. Marcus cried out in feigned innocence: "The New Year has only one hand! How is he to fight me?" The audience laughed, full well aware of Bedwyr's skill with a sword, and guessing his opponent to be untrained and woefully mismatched. Marcus retorted smartly to the good-natured jeers of the spectators; but when Bedwyr casually knocked Marcus's staff aside with his useless arm, Lleu's voice rang out above the rest in a peal of delighted laughter. Marcus whipped around to face him. "I suppose you can do better?" he challenged. He tore the wreath of flowers from his head, crying, "I've been killed eight times today already. Let the New Year fight one who can defend himself!" Faceless still, masked in white linen, he advanced upon Lleu and snatched away the golden circlet to replace it with his own. "A worthy champion for the Old Year!" Marcus announced triumphantly, dragging the protesting Bright One to the center of the floor.

"Pull out your sword, young Harvest Lord,
Defender of the Sun!"

Bedwyr repeated, as Marcus pressed his staff into Lleu's hand. Lleu swallowed his mirth and straightened the wreath he now wore, black hair tousled beneath blossom out of season, dark eyes glinting in a face white with excitement: he stood slender and solitary amid the costumed figures, a single human youth among savages or gods. He said to the audience in confidential tones, "You realize how unfair this is. They've been practicing all evening." There was some laughter at that, but it was hushed, for this would be a duel worth watching.

It went on, and on. Even Bedwyr, who had taught him, could not disarm Lleu son of Artos. The revelers cheered and laughed till they must gasp for breath, feverish in their pleasure. Marcus shouted at last, "You're supposed to let him kill you!"

"Why would anyone do that?" Lleu cried, without a gap in his defense.

"So we can get on with this foolish show and eat," Bedwyr grunted.

Lleu threw down his staff and held his arms out wide, in a comic gesture of frustration and submission. "What must I do, hurl myself upon your blade?" Bedwyr made as though to stab him, and Lleu fell dramatically, taking near as long to die as he had taken to be killed. "Have you finished?" Bedwyr demanded, and to the crowd's delight Lleu answered distinctly, "Oh, very well." He closed his eyes and lay still.

Bedwyr breathed an exaggerated sigh of relief, and Caius turned to him in high fury:

"Wretched cur, what have you done,
So to dispatch my only son?"

Now he turned to the crowd.

"Is there a man so wise in art
That he can quicken fast the slain,
Defy the ordered season's course
And wake this youth to life again?"

Gofan bellowed deeply: "Send for a Magician!"

Now until this moment I had been costumed as were the other rhymers, in a formless suit of leaves and straw, except that my mask was black. Hidden within a little throng of shapeless, faceless men, I had removed the shaggy coat to reveal the black robe underneath. At Gofan's call I stepped into the open space; I held in my right hand the last of the fire sticks from Cathay. Its glittering white core poured heatless sparks over the fierce golden dragon coiled around my wrist. The crowd fell silent.

Into the silence I said quietly, "I am the Magician."

So I stood, unmoving, until the fire stick flickered out. Then Gofan said, "Oh, are you?"

I answered modestly, "Well, some know me as a doctor."

A little breath of laughter rippled through the crowd, a relief.

"What ailments can you cure?" asked Caius, and Gofan added, "More than one or less than two?"

I made the answer.

"I can cure a thousand illnesses that are not there,
And heal a thousand wounds that never were.
I have been praised for miracles from here to Africa!"

Someone laughed.

"I have a bottle in my breast,
A liquor whose clear fire could turn
A glacier to a running stream.
One drop will save your stricken son.

135

"But first I'll have my fee," I added. "Ten silver coins."

Caius asked of Gofan, "Have you any silver?" and Gofan retorted, "Only what can be scraped from the lead mines of the Pennines. There's no ore here but copper." The audience laughed again. Caius turned to me and reported, "He has no silver."

"Then I'll take copper." The ritual payment was made. Caius said with flourish,

"Now try your skill, Magician.
Grant that new life may follow old
When your spell weaves through this hall,
To thrive despite the cold."

I knelt and bent over Lleu, who lay smiling with eyes closed, waiting for the ritual words.

"Into your wounds the golden drops
I pour from our the healing cup—"

He opened his eyes, and nearly choked at what he saw. I smiled down at him faintly, masked in black silk, my hand on his chest heavy with the gold I wore. I finished the verse:

"As death came to the Winter Prince,
So may the Lord of Spring rise up,"

and held my hand to him. He took it defiantly, ghost white, but smiling nonetheless. When the watchers applauded the mock miracle, Lleu turned a handspring and accidentally shed the rhymer's wreath in a shower of red berries and white blossoms. Marcus laughed and handed back to Lleu his own circlet. We chanted the final lines of the pageant:

"Our rhyming is come to a close;
We mean to play no longer here.
May fortune fold this hearth and hold:
So welcome the New Year!"

Lleu did not speak to me again during the celebration that followed. He outdid himself dancing, and even managed to emerge triumphant from a spontaneous wrestling match that developed in a corner of the hall among a few of the boys and young men. He would not look at me, and in the wild throng of dancers and feasters it was simple enough for him to avoid me. But afterward, before I came to you, I found him sitting on the warm floor of the atrium near the brazier, playing with one of the cats.

The gold band he had worn earlier lay at his side, discarded. The low fire shimmered in the cat's eyes and on a few silver threads in Lleu's sleeves and at his throat; he sat alone, head down, very quiet.

"Good night, Prince," I said, for I could not pass by without acknowledging him.

"Medraut!" He let go of the cat, but it did not leave him: it sat next to him on its haunches, rubbing its head against his elbow.

"My lord?" I said, passionless, pausing to wait for his word.

"Medraut, I'm sorry." He ran a hand down the cat's back and then traced the edge of the circlet with his finger, not looking at me. "I mean, for behaving so badly."

"Thank you," I said. I drew a sharp breath and said quietly, harshly, "But, my lord, your apology can do nothing to reverse what you said before your cousins this evening."

"Medraut, I'm sorry, I'm sorry," Lleu pleaded. "Surely they know?"

"They know now," I said.

He rubbed his forehead and murmured, "I feel terrible."

"Oh, little brother, don't waste your time," I whispered.

That silenced him. He gathered himself to stand up, the cat in one arm; he was only on one knee when he dropped it. Then he noticed the gold band on the floor, and bent to pick it up, but in the act of getting to his feet again he dropped that as well. It clattered tinnily on the tesserae, spinning around upon itself before it finally lay still. Lleu put an unsteady hand to his temple, as though confused, and again bent to retrieve the circlet. I took him by the shoulders and made him straighten. "Have you had too much to drink?" I asked.

"Hardly anything," he said. But his eyes seemed depthless pools of black water, and the skin around them had a tight, bruised look to it.

"Look at me," I said, and drew him close to one of the tall lamps. He winced at the sudden bright light in his eyes and turned his face away; I took hold of his chin and turned him back to the light. "Let me see your eyes." I scrutinized Lleu carefully in the lamplight, and felt his hot cheeks, and counted the slow pulse in his throat.

Ai, Godmother, how?

I told him in a voice without expression, "She seems to have poisoned you again."

After a pause, Lleu cried softly, "Oh, curse her!" in a high, sharp voice, like a bird screaming.

I said slowly, "You will be in some pain later tonight, I think."

"Can't you do anything?" he asked.

"I can," I answered, looking straight into his eyes. He could hardly stand steadily, and his skin was so pale it seemed faintly cast with blue. As I turned to go I deliberately stepped on his circlet: I kept my foot there for half a moment and added, without looking back, "But I am not going to."

His voice when he spoke next was uncertain and low, but he dared to say, "Must I command you?"

I shook my head in disbelief and answered quietly, "You must never command me." I left him so, alone with his glittering mosaic in the dying firelight.

XI

The Prince Betrayed

The woman set to watch you was asleep, nodding over the garment she had been hemming. "Have you—," I began to ask, but you shook your head and put a discreet finger to your lips. "Speak low. I've done nothing to her."

"You have to another!"

"That was for you."

"For me!" I laughed. "Well, thank you. But no more of it, Godmother."

"No." You sliced back and forth across the floor, exactly like one of your caged wildcats, I the hare or moorhen that ought to be cowering in a corner and hoping you would not notice that I was there. But I was there of my own will. I waited, waited, wondering how you would strike.

You were thinking hard, fitting what you had to say to words that only I could understand should someone else happen to hear you. "I want you to hunt for me," you said at last.

"What quarry?" I asked cautiously.

"I want the sun." Then you fell silent for a time, and ceased pacing as you cloaked your treachery in words mysterious as mummers' costumes. "If you were a prisoner in blackness, in the cold, if you were an exile in a place of chill and darkness, you would wish that the sun were yours to command: then you could have light and warmth to your whim and pleasure. The sun in your hand, *the sun for a ransom*—then see the oppressive shadows bend to your will!"

You stopped, facing me, your hands in fists. "The sun," I repeated, my voice flat. "How am I to get you the sun?"

You hissed in disgust, "You stupid boy!" and turned away, to strip leaves from the little lemon tree Ginevra had set in the window, and then to tear them to shreds between fierce fingers.

I hissed in answer, "Godmother, I do know what you mean." You stood silent, so still that I could hear the slight patter on the tiles as the torn leaves fell from your fingers. I said, "I am pledged to serve the light."

"You are pledged to me first."

"As I am pledged to both, I may decide not to fail either trust." But I waited to hear what else you might say. "Why should I hunt for you more than another?"

You did not speak aloud. For answer your lips formed one single silent word, which I heard as clearly as if you had shouted it: "Kingship."

"Temptress," I taunted, tempted.

You whispered, "The boy outshines you as surely as the noon sun outshines the moon in eclipse. You know it; you hate him for it. When I tested your loyalty last summer your defense of him was wretched."

"I had not known it was a test."

"You were so protective of me, or so reluctant to lose me, that it took you a week to tell his father," you said dryly. "If I had meant to kill him—"

"Be still!" I lashed out. "Your door is open wide. If anyone should come—"

"What would happen? How would I be made more of a prisoner than I already am?" You spoke quickly and quietly in desperate anger, heedless of who might hear. "What a fruitless journey I made when I came here—my brother will not speak to me, and I am not even allowed to join the household for their Midwinter's feast. As soon as the weather breaks Gwalchmei is to take me back to Ratae Coritanorum for the rest of the winter, and in the spring Artos will see that I go back to the Orcades. Out of sight, out of mind. Gods, I am tired of the endless winter nights, the dark and the cold and the boredom! This exile will drive me mad, Medraut. If Artos will not return to me the old freedom, the old power, I will fight him for it. I want to hold and hurt his beautiful young favorite, his darling; I want to see that proud, bright child trapped as one would cage a little bird, helpless as a wren or robin beating vain and desperate wings against bars of my making. I mean to rape and ruin what Artos loves best until he too bends broken to my will."

I could make no answer.

"The sun for my ransom," you repeated, low. "And for yours. After New Year's, in Ratae Coritanorum. Bring me the sun, and Artos will follow to do my bidding. Agravain knows, he is also pledged to me. He will go with you."

"I prefer to hunt alone," I said.

"I don't trust you alone."

I shrugged indifferently. "Nobody trusts me."

"My darling!" You spoke without tenderness, your voice smooth and black as tarnished silver. You twisted your arms around my neck and gripped my hair in your fists so that I could not move my head. "You have not agreed. Give me an answer."

"Have I a choice? You are using me," I cried out softly.

"I am helping you!" But your voice was cruel and cold.

"I do not want your help," I whispered in fury. "I am the one you hurt when you are angry, whatever you might threaten otherwise. It is I that you have crippled."

"Oh, you are not so damaged as that."

I said in anger, "What of the damage to my soul?"

"Your soul is your own responsibility," you answered without patience.

"How can you make light of what you have done to me? You have left all my body scarred in little ways, my back, my throat, my hands. There is a scar inside my mouth where once you stabbed a hairpin through my cheek. I am like a ruined piece of parchment scrawled over and over again with your name, so many times it has become illegible. Even in sleep I am not free of you!" I spoke on edge between a whisper and a scream, standing taut and motionless while your fists tightened in my hair.

"You have not scarred me," you answered through shut teeth. "But do you think I do not dream of you?"

Then kissed me.

For a moment, half a moment, I was lost. There was only sheer pleasure, and desire, and a kind of relief. But half a moment. Then I tore myself away, leaving you clutching fistful of my hair, and fell over a footstool which went to

143

splinters beneath my weight. I sat graceless and trembling among the shards of ivory as you stooped hawklike over me, and then I heard Lleu's clear voice speak my name.

"Medraut."

The guardswoman had started up when I fell. Now she came quickly to my aid, exclaiming in consternation; I was hardly aware of her. All my attention was on Lleu, standing in the doorway. He was on his way to his own bedroom and had not been here long, but he must have seen enough to turn his stomach. The brilliant contempt in his eyes was directed only at me. "You disgust me," he said quietly.

I gasped a little, unable to speak, still trembling. I do not know what you looked at or saw, or what the other woman did. I saw only Lleu, and heard only Lleu as he repeated coldly, "You disgust me."

So he pronounced judgment. The Bright One, the sun lord.

It all took me at once: my father's distrust, the shame and horror of the copper mines, Lleu's denouncement of me before your other children. His clear young voice demanding obedience even as he stood poisoned and hoping for my mercy. The wooden sword held at my throat.

I spat at his feet. He stared at me with wide eyes, unbelieving, then turned away and left us without another word.

What I did now was of my own choosing, not out of any loyalty that I must break or affirm. I said bitterly, "Godmother, I will hunt for you."

The weather turned the next day, and barely a day after that Artos sent you back to Ratae Coritanorum with

Gwalchmei as your escort. As Christmas approached Goewin said to me, "Please, Medraut, can't you forgive Lleu? He's only thoughtless, not evil. The two of you haven't spoken since Midwinter's."

"Agravain and I are going hunting the week after Christmas," I answered. "I will take Lleu if he will come."

"Well, you know how he likes to hunt," she said with a crooked smile. "I'll try to convince him to go with you."

"Goewin, why don't you come as well?" I said. "Then he can't refuse."

"Would you have me?" she asked, surprised and pleased. "I'd like to go. Thank you, Medraut."

We left Camlan two days past Christmas, four days behind you. But I told Agravain we should allow you time to travel, so we set out north instead of south. Artos had given his permission and blessing for us to go; Lleu had never been on a long winter journey, and it would be for him another test, another lesson. Another step toward kingship.

We rode through the deer park, and passed through the gap in the peaks south of the high moor where I had taken the twins two summers before. Then we were in hilly, empty forest, with the moors rising around us. The forest close to Camlan is cultivated, but in the Pennines it is wild, mostly trackless, haunted by boar and bear and wolf. The day began gray and dark and never truly grew light. At noon when we might have stopped to eat it began to rain, a cold, soaking rain mixed with sleet. It was warmer to continue riding. By afternoon we had come over twenty slow miles; now we rode along a valley beneath a bare ridge whose peak had shrugged off layers of black, broken rock. "I know where we are," said Goewin. "That hill with the landslip is Shivering Mountain. There used to be lead mines here."

"There are still caves," I said. "We often use them for shelter on long hunts. I know a place we can stay; it will be full darkness soon."

Relieved at the promise of a dry place to sleep, Agravain and Lleu began to fling congenial insults back and forth. Agravain boasted that he surely sought bigger quarry than Lleu could ever hope to bring down; Goewin rode with me companionably. I could not look at any of them, wanting to laugh at Agravain's gibes, but held in check by my own hidden treachery.

I found the cave, which was dry and warmer than outside. The opening was out of the wind, and there was an overhanging rock near the entrance where a small fire could be protected from the rain without polluting the air of the inner chamber. We fed and blanketed the horses, and unloaded our own satchels. Lleu untied the bundles of spears and bows we had bound to the saddles; he dropped them just inside the cave's entrance with a clatter, and Agravain laughed. Lleu said ruefully, "I'm tired."

"I too," I acknowledged. My throat burned and ached. "Agravain, if you build a fire I'll heat some wine."

I came inside after the others. The cave was lit by the fire and the lanterns Agravain had set about the floor. I shared out the drink carelessly; Lleu nodded thanks when I filled his horn and did not notice that I had laced his warm wine with nightshade. Words from the rhymers' pageant suddenly struck through my mind, but twisted:

Into your wine the golden drops
I pour from out the poisoned cup
As death comes to the Winter Prince. . . .

I choked and turned away to strip myself of sodden shirt
and jacket, feeling flushed with excitement and fierce determination. Goewin said sharply, "Are you all right,
Medraut?"

She had noticed my clenched and shaking hands. I
laughed at her over my shoulder, freely, and tried to stretch
away the tension in my arms and back. The ceiling was too
low for me to stand erect. "It has been a hard day."

"Well, yes," she agreed.

"There's food in the large satchel, Goewin," I said. "We
shouldn't eat much." I went to stand outside the entrance to
the cave, where I did not have to stoop. The sleet had turned
to snow. I watched the dark outline of Shivering Mountain
disappear as the light faded quickly, until all I could see were
the swirling flakes just beyond the firelight.

"God's sake, Medraut, you'll kill yourself," Goewin said
behind me. "You aren't even wearing a shirt. Come in."

I ducked below the entrance to join the others and sat
across from Lleu. Agravain shared out strips of salted meat
and dried fruit.

"It's snowing, isn't it?" Lleu asked. His eyes seemed
hooded, dark and strange.

"Yes," I told him. "But no fear, Bright One; we've food
and furs and shelter, and there is little wind." I reached out to
push damp strands of his hair off his forehead. His hand
moved aimlessly, as though he meant to turn away my touch,

but could not connect mind with movement. He was struggling to stay awake. I coughed and turned my face away; I could not bear to watch him.

"Medraut—"

I do not remember which of them spoke my name.

It was Lleu who got to his feet, unsteadily and laboriously, but with a courage and composure that I had not expected of him. He stood before me, but I could not face him upright without striking my head against the ceiling. I did not try to rise.

"Have you drugged me?" Lleu demanded, his voice even, his hands tremorous. "I was not so very weary before we ate!"

"Yes," I whispered without remorse. "I have."

"You promised me!" he cried.

"What did I promise? Do you remember precisely what I said?"

"No!" he answered angrily. "What, then? It was two years ago, and I was half-asleep."

Goewin spoke now in a dull, chill voice, staring at nothing as she accurately repeated the promise I had made. "He said he would never again send you to sleep at any time you might be ill or hurt. You aren't ill or hurt." She whispered through her teeth: "He keeps his promises."

"But why do this? So I'll sleep well? Medraut, it isn't fair! I'm not an invalid." He sat down heavily and suddenly, unable to keep his feet any longer.

"I have finished with fairness," I said. "I have done this to put you at my mercy."

"At your mercy?" Goewin echoed. Her face was gray. "What in heaven's name are you doing?"

The four of us sat staring at one another. Agravain watched me fiercely through the screen of his unbound copper hair, waiting for my word, and it was as though you watched me through another's eyes. Goewin said in a high voice, "My lord and brother, give me a straight answer!"

"I am under command," I said.

Agravain could no longer hold silent. "My mother means to use the prince of Britain as a hostage; we are to bring him to her in Ratae Coritanorum."

"Me!" Lleu breathed.

"You are the prince of Britain," Agravain uttered derisively.

Lleu sneered in return, "Why would I ever take you seriously, Agravain?"

I asked gently, "Can you lift your hands, Lleu?"

He could not. He turned to his sister with a look of horror, and turned too quickly; he lost his balance. Goewin caught him. "Medraut, you're lying," she said in desperation.

I replied quietly, "I never lie."

"But why have you brought me?" she asked.

Agravain answered, "You are to carry the message back to your father." He continued recklessly, "My mother hates her brother, she hates his children, the two of you. She hates the unspoken exile she is kept in. She wants freedom and power."

I said in a still voice, "Lleu is freedom and power."

"She will use the prince as a playing piece to bargain with," Agravain continued. "His life, his body unharmed, for whatever she desires."

"And why do you serve her in defiance of the high king?" Goewin challenged, her voice still high, but steady.

"I would serve her in defiance of anyone," he told her with passionate fervor. "And the high king is not her master, after all, only her brother."

"Oh, devotion!" Goewin scoffed, holding Lleu upright as he sagged against her shoulder. "Then is Gwalchmei in this as well?"

"Not he." Agravain laughed. "Not the newest of the high king's Comrades! He will be on his way back to Camlan by the time we reach Ratae Coritanorum."

"But you, Medraut—" Goewin began. Then she and Lleu both began to speak at once, neither of them willing or perhaps even able to believe that I could fail them.

"Has Lleu betrayed you so terribly?"

"I have entrusted my life to you!"

"Are you not pledged to serve him?"

"You are my *brother*."

"Why on earth would you do such a thing for Morgause?"

"Because," I answered savagely, "she will demand that Artos make me king in place of Lleu."

"Why would he do that?" Goewin said coldly.

"What will he do otherwise, with Lleu's life in the balance?" I questioned. "I think he loves his youngest child too dearly to refuse. Besides, what has he to lose by complying? Pride, perhaps. It is his own error that keeps me from the kingship, not anything I have done. I am older, stronger, wiser than Lleu; I am liked and admired by the Comrades. If Artos refuses he will have lost both of us. He will not put Britain in such jeopardy."

"He has me still, without either of you," Goewin snarled, "and I am quite capable of reigning."

"Do you hunger for the kingship too?" I laughed, too hard, and began to cough. "Join us, then. If Artos refuses, you and I can kill the prince together."

Goewin hurled her drinking horn at my face; it glanced off my cheek and cracked against the stone wall. Agravain held her back, and Lleu fell forward with chest and cheek against the floor. He fought to right himself, and managed to bring his arms beneath him so that he could raise his head and shoulders.

"You speak so lightly of killing!" Goewin flung at me, trying to break free. "You are no murderer!"

"Indeed I am," I said grimly, "several times over, and by no accident."

Goewin tore herself from Agravain's grasp and flew at me, snatching for the hunting knife that I still wore at my side. "Ah, no, Princess," I said, and seized one of her wrists as I drew the dagger myself. "You are like Lleu: quick, skillful, but not very strong."

Goewin tried to wrench her arm free, but could not fight very well on her knees in the small space with Lleu sprawled between us. She spat, "Obviously you think more of his strength than you do of mine, or you'd have drugged both of us."

"Goewin," I cautioned with the knife raised, "be still."

"Oh, cut my throat! I dare you!"

"Not yours," I said, and still gripping her wrist, pressed the blade against Lleu's neck. His head sank. "Now, be still."

Goewin went limp. "You would not."

"I will not kill him, no," I granted. "At least, not now. But if you do not stop struggling I will hurt him."

"Take him, then," she cried. "Ah, God, you make me

sick. Cold and aloof as you are, I trusted you more deeply than I would my father, counted your word more binding than I would my own. Soulless viper! Take him! How can I stand in your way now?"

I let her go. She got up and stormed outside into the dark, the snow, the wilderness.

"Shall I bring her back?" Agravain asked.

"Let her be. There is nowhere for her to go."

Lleu whispered raspingly, "You would not have hurt me."

"Are you with us yet, Bright One?" I said in wonder. "You must be fighting as you have never fought before. That dose was stronger than any the queen of the Orcades has ever given you."

"You would not hurt me," Lleu repeated, and with his final fading consciousness reached out to take my crippled hand in his, unafraid, blindly trusting and certain. I could not understand what he tried to say. His fearlessness puzzled me, and I sat silent, gazing down at the dark head and slim hand that clasped my own, wondering.

Goewin came back inside, and without a word helped me to strip Lleu of his wet clothes and to wrap him in furs and blankets for the night. Agravain packed away the remaining food and put out all the lanterns but one; then the three of us joined Lleu in sleep.

I dozed in fits and starts, tangled in monotonous dreams of riding and moors and rain. In the middle of the night I began to cough uncontrollably, yet could not wake; I lay wretchedly gasping for air, unaware of where I was or who was with me. Then a gentle hand shook my shoulder, and a gentle, concerned voice said, "Medraut. Medraut, sit up, it'll stop."

The voice was insistent. The hand worked its way beneath my back to help me up, and I could breathe again. Goewin knelt by me, holding me upright, gazing at me anxiously. "Shall I get you something to drink?" she asked.

I said at last, softly, "You are very kind, Goewin."

"Oh." She crept to the bags and satchels and poured water for me. "Well, you sounded so awful."

"Think where you are," I said.

She blinked. The lantern flickered, burning low, and sent waves of light across her face. "I know where I am," she said.

"Why help me, then? To win my favor?"

"You woke me up," she answered irritably. "You sounded as though you couldn't breathe. Are you ill?" She touched my forehead briefly with cool fingers and said, "You're burning!"

"Always," I said darkly.

"No," she said, and drew back from me a little, not sure what I meant. "You've a fever."

"I know," I said scornfully.

"For how long?"

"Since early this evening."

"Don't go," she said.

"I must. My mother—"

I stopped, flushed: I, who never spoke a word more than I meant to speak. After a long moment Goewin said slowly, "Do you ever call her mother?"

"I don't," I answered shortly. "But she is."

"What hold has she over you besides that?"

I stared at her. "What *hold*?" I coughed again, near

laughter, incredulous. "Isn't that enough? You're not blind, Goewin."

"But you don't want to do this!"

"How could you know what I want?" I said. "Under her orders I can take vengeance on your beautiful brother and let the blame fall on her."

Goewin said forcefully, "Revenge for what?" Neither of us spoke for a few moments. At last Goewin ventured, "Then you'd torture Lleu and turn over what's left to her? That would please her as much as if she did it herself, wouldn't it? Either way you are seduced—"

"No!" I burst out, so violently that Agravain stirred in his sleep. My fingers had gone taut and white around the small horn cup Goewin had given me. "I follow my own will!"

"Then why are you doing this?" Goewin pressed.

I coughed and pushed my hair back from my face; it was dry now, and tangled. Goewin took the cup from me and watched me in apprehension. I said, "You of anyone should understand."

"I understand your mother," she said unexpectedly. "I understand her all too well. I live in constant fear that I will be kept prisoner as she is, because I am dangerous and powerful, and because I am a woman. I would not betray Lleu even if I wanted to; he is my sole ally, my one defense against such a fate. But you, Medraut, you have been offered the regency of his kingdom, you have power in your hand. So *why*?"

I drew my fingers across Lleu's cheek and lips as though I were touching something beautiful and delicate, an exotic flower, a piece of old silk, the skeleton of a leaf. "For a word. For my father's word. For something I want Artos to say. I want him to admit, before all, that it is his own iniquity that keeps me from the kingship. That the shame is his, not mine." I paused, my fingertips trembling above Lleu's still face, and then went on speaking as though to myself, as though she were not there. "And I want Lleu to be afraid of me, to know and admit to my authority. I want—" I hesitated again, lost. I did not know what I wanted. "Lleu's grown so confident and cruel."

"He's not cruel!" Goewin said.

"He is," I said. "He is ever conscious of his beauty, his power. And he never quite stops sneering at me for my being so . . . scarred.

"I might end by killing him," I finished bitterly. "I would do it if I had a reason, if I were given the command. He would deserve it."

"He would not. You fret like a jealous child," Goewin whispered roughly. "I am as much in the way of your kingship as Lleu is. Take me in his place. Let him go."

"I couldn't take you," I said slowly. "I am too much afraid of what I might do to you."

"What could be more terrible than anything you might do to Lleu?" she asked.

I looked at her hard and straight, perplexed, unable to believe her so naive. Then I took her face between my fevered palms and held her close, so that we must look directly at one another. My hands moved down her throat, across her shoulders, until at last they were cupped gently beneath her breasts; and then she knew what I might do to her. "I am your sister," she said.

"You see how it happens," I said, and let her go.

She sat still for a moment, her eyes lowered, as though in

prayer. Then she carefully set the horn cup on the floor away from us, and moved back to her place between Lleu and the cave wall. She lay on her back with her eyes closed and said in an icy voice, "If you don't bring Lleu back alive and unharmed I'll kill you, I swear it, surely, I will find a way to kill you."

"I fear you as little as you fear me," I whispered.

XII
Peak and Forest

Morning, now. Lleu woke up and was sick. I began to help him dress, but he shrank from the touch of my hot hands over his bare arms and back; Goewin, watching, barked out, "Let him go!" I glanced at her with half a grin, but shrugged and gave Lleu his dry shirt and jacket and then drew away. Afterward he crouched dejectedly next to the fire with his head in his hands, not yet able to eat or to stand. Goewin said to me severely, "You who never lie, have you thought what quarry you will bring away as proof of this week's hunting?"

Lleu raised his head with an effort and answered in quiet, "Has he not?"

I took Goewin outside to speak to her alone. I wanted to be certain she knew her way back to Camlan, and there were other things I must instruct her in as well. "When you get home," I said, "stay there. Persuade your father not to come searching for us, nor to try to apprehend his sister in Ratae Coritanorum. He will have to wait for further word before he moves to save his child."

"Why would he wait," Goewin asked, "once he knows what you intend?"

"He won't know that," I said. "I will not follow the road. I cannot risk a direct route."

"Oh, Medraut," she sighed. "Where will you go?"

The high moors and valley below us lay blanketed in snow, several inches deep. The clouds were thin, but covered the whole sky, so that the sun glinted weak and silver through a misty screen and gave neither warmth nor much light. It was enough, though. "Today I mean to strike out across open country."

"Where you can find your way by following the sun and the sound of water, and no one will be able to find you."

"Just so."

"Then all I can do—"

"Obey my word."

Goewin left before we did. I made her take Lleu's horse as well as her own, so that she was forced to travel slowly, and so that Lleu must remain dependent on me. The Bright One, my prisoner, betrayed his fear only in the way he clung to his sister when she embraced him in farewell: his face hidden against her shoulder, his hands clenched in fierce and frantic fists.

After she had gone we too set out, descending through a narrow pass with steep, rocky sides as though we traveled among the bones of the land itself; rocks tore through the snow like dark, fleshless elbows and knees. After this stark gully we emerged onto a gently sloping moor, still in sight of the distinct black ridge called Shivering Mountain. Here I turned across the moor that spread before us, smooth and white and apparently endless. Beneath the snow the ground was treacherously uneven. We journeyed slowly, more slowly than we had the day before. When we lost sight of Shivering Mountain it was difficult to have any idea of where we were, for all directions led to the same seamless white horizon. We passed a high point on the barren slope and continued down a similar expanse of emptiness.

We stopped to eat in the shelter of the fallen entrance to a disused mine. Within our sight the horizon was at last broken by a few low, unnatural mounds of earth that rose from the level ground, ancient burial chambers or ruined huts. "Where are we?" Agravain asked. We had said little to each other during the morning's journey; the wind made it difficult to speak when we were in the open.

"Are you lost too?" Lleu murmured. "I thought you were leading this venture."

"Where are we, Medraut?" Agravain repeated.

"Old Moor. This way is shorter."

Agravain said, "It's more difficult."

Lleu looked up at me, silent. He frowned a little, as though he were trying to map his way through a fog, trying to fathom what I was thinking.

"It is more difficult," I acknowledged. "But also more beautiful."

"You make no sense," Lleu said.

I was too hot, arms and legs aching with fever. I longed to feel the cold I could see all around. Whenever we stopped to rest I faced the wind and stood gazing across the still, colorless plains, my back straight and my cloak and scarf loose.

When we walked to let the horses rest, or when the ground grew rough and we dismounted to fight our way on foot through the concealed pockmarks in the land, Agravain and Lleu sheltered against the animals' warm bodies; but I always moved to windward, facing the cold unafraid, desiring it. Once I plunged a hand into a snowdrift and rubbed the melting crystals over my forehead and through my hair. Agravain watched me curiously and then looked away, embarrassed by such eccentricity. But Lleu suddenly reached up to dry my forehead with the end of my scarf, and said quietly, "Don't do that."

As the day wore on we left the moor and entered one of the narrow, forested dales, following a trickle of icy water that had somehow cut a cleft into the land. Snow clung to the stark and leafless twigs like blossom out of season. In the gray, dimming light I could not tell whether it was snowing yet again, or if the seldom flakes were only drifting from the branches overhead. Among the bare trees were tracts of pine that were once farmed for timber; here we stopped for the night, under the shelter of an evergreen whose heavy, snow-laden needles dragged the spreading limbs almost to the ground. There was little snow beneath the tree, and the ground was too frozen to be damp. When night fell we built a fire. The tree made a protective tent around us, and we were able to heat wine and toast bread, while the smoke drifted and curled into the dark branches above. When we had finished with eating Lleu huddled close to the fire, scowling at the frigid night with his cloak wrapped tightly about his shoulders and his scarf swathed over his head beneath his hood. "It's too cold to sleep," he said.

Agravain responded in scorn and wonder, "You're still

cold?" We were well equipped, both with furs and with blankets of thick, good wool.

"Aren't you?" Lleu snapped back at him. "I didn't say I was cold. I said it's too cold to sleep."

"Then don't sleep," Agravain replied without sympathy.

Lleu started suddenly, as though a chill had passed over him; the shadow of a ghost or an idea. He rose and began to peel off the layers of wool in which he had shrouded himself, until he stood straight and shivering with his hands on his hips and his cloak thrown back over his shoulders. "If I'm lucky, maybe the two of you will freeze to death overnight."

"Never count on luck."

Agravain glanced at me and held silent as I spoke, his eyes glinting in the firelight as he waited for me to deal in some crushing way with Lleu's insurrection.

"I won't," Lleu answered quietly. Then with the speed and sudden agility of all his training as dancer and swordsman, he vaulted toward the carefully stacked weapons and seized his own small bow and a fistful of arrows. We both leaped toward him, and he brandished the arrows at us as though he held a dagger or a flaming torch. By chance he scratched the back of Agravain's outstretched hand, and as Agravain paused to curse and wince, I stumbled in his path.

Lleu dropped the arrows. In the moment of our hesitation he strung his bow; when I regained my balance he stood with the bow drawn and trained in our direction. The other bows and spears lay at his feet, as did the arrows. He burst out in fury, "Don't either of you move. By God, Medraut, you taught me to kill, and I will do it, if I must, to save myself." His face was pallid, but his hands did not tremble. His bow was bent to its extent, the bowstring taut as he could stretch it. He stood close enough to either of us that there was scarcely any need for him to take aim; all he must do is loose his arrow. Agravain reached for his hunting knife, and Lleu sent the arrow plowing into the hard earth near his cousin's foot. He snatched for another and notched it to his bow with a speed and accuracy I never anticipated. "I cannot shoot like Medraut," he said, voice and hand steady, steady. "If I try to come closer than that I might hit you. Don't force me to try." He was in desperate, deadly earnest.

"I want your daggers. Keep them sheathed." Agravain unfastened his hunting knife and tossed it with angry reluctance at his cousin's feet. I did not move, sure that I could regain control of the situation in some way. Lleu turned the drawn bow toward me. "Hunter turns quarry," he said softly. "I do not like this game, Medraut, my brother."

"You play it very well," I answered, still without moving.

"I will train this arrow at your throat for the rest of the night if you don't obey me," Lleu said through his teeth. "How you scorn me! You count too much on your superior strength. You wield it over my head like an executioner's sword. That you are stronger than me does not make you better, or more ruthless, or wiser."

"Show me your superior wit," I said with disdain.

"I am," he protested, laughing. "Why did you not bind me, or guard your weapons? Did you imagine I would deliver myself with docile acceptance into the cruel and terrifying hands of the queen of the Orcades? Give me your dagger. And mine, you have them both."

"I will not," I said patiently. "Will you really stand there all night?"

He suddenly turned on Agravain and launched another

arrow at his cousin, and drew his bow again. Agravain stared at Lleu with wide, angry eyes. "I care less for this fawning minion than I do for you, Medraut. Don't make me hurt him. Give me the daggers."

"Do it," Agravain hissed.

So I had threatened Goewin the night before, knowing that she would do my bidding rather than let me harm her brother. I threw the knives contemptuously at Lleu's feet, more in the spirit of one accepting a challenge than because I cared for Agravain's safety. Lleu said, "Now, Agravain, come here. I want you to burn the other bows. Don't touch the spears."

Efficiently and effectively, Lleu disposed of all the weapons we had brought with us except for his own bow, the hunting knives, and a little hand ax which he used to destroy the spears. He kept only as many arrows as he could comfortably carry in a quiver. When he had seen to this purge of arms, he relaxed his guard and once more sat across from us by the fire; his face was still without color, but despite his evident fear he was confident, excited.

"We are vulnerable," Agravain said sullenly, "to any beast or man that might choose to attack us."

Lleu laughed again. "Oh, the bears are all asleep. We are safe enough by firelight, don't you think, Medraut? I am no faultless marksman, but I have a steady hand. As to men, who were you expecting to meet in this wild wood, in dead of winter?"

"What do you mean to do now?" I asked quietly.

Lleu pulled up his hood and wrapped his cloak about him, the heat of his rebellion wearing thin. He propped his chin on his fists, with his elbows resting on his knees, and stared at the fire. "I don't know where we are. You know that." He spoke slowly, thinking. "I want you to guide me back across the moor we crossed today, back to Shivering Mountain, where I can find my own way. From there we will return to Camlan, and my father can charge you or forgive you as he sees fit."

"You will need a better plan than that," I said. "I am not turning back."

"You are. You will."

"Why? Will you kill me if I refuse your command?"

Lleu narrowed his eyes, staring at the fire as he realized his dilemma. He said slowly, "I can't. Without you I am lost."

I turned to Agravain sardonically. "You must admire his honesty."

"Don't mock me, Medraut!" Lleu cried. "You are at my mercy!"

I looked at him directly, shaking my head. "Not entirely. You are at mine, as well."

This was so clear, so indisputable, that he did not argue. He sat in glaring silence for a few moments and presently asked, "What then? What will you do instead?"

"Two or three days south of here lies the road that runs to Ratae Coritanorum. If you follow it north it will lead you toward Shining Ridge, near Camlan. We will continue southward; and when we reach the road, if you are still free, you can turn home yourself. If not, we will take the road south."

"If I am still free!" Lleu repeated. "Why shouldn't I be?"

"How will you keep us from seizing you in your sleep; how will you remain in control of two who are stronger than you, by yourself, for as many days as it takes to reach your destination?"

Lleu turned from one to the other of us, his expression caught between a puzzled frown and a mask of mounting dismay at the thought of the ordeal that lay before him. "I will not sleep. I will guard you."

"Your own strength may fail you by the time we reach the road," I warned him.

"I see no other course," he admitted.

He kept awake all night. Agravain slept soundly; but I woke every few hours, watching for a slip in Lleu's guard, a flaw in his defense. That first night, there was none. He talked to the horses and sang to himself, and toward dawn he walked the perimeter of our campsite in thoughtful silence. There will be time, I told myself. Be patient with him. He will break himself before we reach the road.

It was gray again in the morning. While Agravain and I struck camp, Lleu stormed idly back and forth beneath the trees, driven with nervous energy. Once he tripped over a root hidden beneath the snow, and I dropped a pile of furs thinking to catch him off-guard. But he was on his feet before I could reach him: bruised and annoyed at his clumsiness, who was so light, so agile by nature. His eyes were bright and weary at the same time, alert and bloodshot. He kicked at the remains of the fire till the ashes flew about his feet like soft gray moths.

There was no sign that any other man or woman had ever set foot in this place. We still followed the same little river as it wound farther and farther south, but throughout the day we did not see a single cottage distant among the bare trees, or any kind of track through the forest. Lleu would not eat food that I prepared, wary lest I try to poison him again. Determination made him bold; he shot two rabbits before evening fell, and skinned and dressed them himself. We had plenty to eat that night. But I was fast in the grip of fever and ate only toasted bread and dried fruit. I had no appetite for meat.

We camped in a little clearing and brushed aside the snow until we had an area large enough to spread our blankets and build a fire. After we had eaten we sat about the fire as we had the night before. Lleu set aside his bow and ceased to watch me as he cleaned his hunting knife; and so without warning I snatched for the dagger.

He slashed the knife beyond my reach, holding it away from his body like a torch. He held steady, not moving, eyeing me distrustfully. He knew that resistance kept him alert; he did not consider how it drained him.

I dove at him again. We both got to our feet and struggled together for a moment; I tried to seize my own dagger from his belt, but he had bound it in its sheath. I broke away from him in disgust and stepped aside into the snow and shadow beyond the clearing we had made. Lleu would have let the matter end; but now Agravain scrambled to his feet and caught Lleu's arms from behind. Lleu rested a prisoner for a few moments, panting a little, as I stood poised and motionless outside the circle of firelight. Agravain could do little more than hold him, for Lleu was armed with the shining steel that we had both sought to win from him. I thought to wear Lleu down, to tire him out. I waited for him.

Lleu suddenly snapped out of Agravain's hold and spun away, and I sprang to meet him. He sheathed his knife and watched me cautiously, not sure what I meant to do. As he hesitated I threw my weight against his chest and shoulders, trying to knock him off-balance. He kept his feet, but I caught and held him with such ferocity that even he could not break free. I drove my young brother to his knees, then bore him to the ground in a twisted heap beneath me, face down in the snow, sobbing and gasping in fury and defeat. I held him there and said to Agravain, "Bind his hands."

I toyed with Lleu's hair with one hand. When he tried to raise his head I held him down without mercy, so that he must lie with one cheek burning against the snow, the cold crystals melting a little when he breathed. "I don't want to hurt you," I told him softly. "But so help me, Bright One, I am going to prove to you my power." Lleu lay quivering with rage and humiliation, while Agravain dragged his cousin's arms behind his back and lashed his wrists together so fiercely that Lleu gave a little gasp of pain.

"Loosen that," I told Agravain.

My compassion undid me. When Agravain unfastened the knots he had made, Lleu somersaulted beyond our reach, shedding arrows from the quiver he still wore, and snatched up his bow. On one knee in the snow he fastened one of his remaining arrows to the bow. "I am not a pawn!" he cried. "I am not a precious stone to be fought over, stolen and bartered and tossed from hand to hand!" He drew a long, trembling breath, and said in a calmer voice, "Ah, go to sleep, Agravain. Think how much less alert I'll be tomorrow. Put the arrows down!"

Agravain stalked back to the fire, where he cocooned himself in furs and seemed to settle to sleep. I watched as Lleu got to his feet and collected the scattered arrows. He dusted the snow from his hair and clothes, then folded a blanket around his laden shoulders and resumed his place by the fire. He sighed. "Medraut, is it lack of power that makes you bound to do this? Surely Morgause cannot offer you more than Artos."

"It is power over you that I crave more than anything, and Artos will never grant me that," I answered in quiet, sitting by him. "You cannot know how I envy you your youth, your beauty, your father's love for you."

He said then, with disarming irrelevance, "Tell me about Africa."

"Africa!" I laughed. "There is nothing to tell that you haven't heard already."

"I like to hear you speak of it."

He said that, armed against me and sitting in my shadow, with the prospect of another sleepless night ahead of him. I closed my eyes and thought of roosters crowing in the early morning, and the smell of charcoal cooking fires. The dirt, the dust, the unreflecting drab of undyed muslin, the women selling water from clay pots they carried on their backs. The crowds in the noisy marketplace, vendors hawking goats and peppers; and the feeling always that I was a foreigner manifest, never able to hide my white hair and white face. A cold stranger from a cold country.

"When I would walk in the streets of Aksum," I said, "I would attract a host of beggars. It was because I was dressed well, but also because I was so different. Even in Deva people look askance at my pale hair. In Aksum my very skin was unnatural."

Lleu watched me, fixedly biting his lip.

I asked, "Do you remember the lepers described in the Christian testaments?"

He nodded.

"The beggars in Aksum were all sick, or mad. They were eyeless and limbless and filthy."

He cried out, "But you were happy there!"

"Aye." I leaned forward to place another branch on the fire, stirring sparks skyward. "Well, Kidane's house was large and cool, with white walls and a courtyard open to the sky. Turunesh kept doves and parrots."

"What did she look like?" Lleu asked.

"You question like an old woman!"

He frowned and tossed his head, and said, "Don't tell me, then."

"She was 'very dark, but comely,'" I told him softly, thinking too of the evenings over the old books, hymns chanted, stories told. "'Like the tents of Kedar, like the curtains of Solomon.'"

We both sat silent, gazing at the fire, while the sweet words of the Song of Songs echoed on the cold and quiet air. Lleu whispered then, "How would she admire you if she learned of this week's hunting?"

I whispered in return, "She would not admire it."

"Did you love her? Have you ever loved anything?"

Yes. Yes. All the wrong things. The hunt, and darkness, and winter, and you, Godmother.

"Oh, be careful, little brother," I breathed. "You are hurling your slight weight against a very thin scale of ice."

"I am chancing for my freedom in any way I can," he answered.

169

He sat awake and watched all through that night.

The morning came gray and changeless. We traveled on foot through still more bare, deserted forest; Lleu walked in a private haze of exhaustion. Snow covered the trees and forest floor as far as could be seen, and drifted across our vision. There was only soft light, the light one dreams by, gray clouds, or snow, or blue shadows, but never the true light of the sun. In the afternoon we left the dale and struck out over another stretch of empty moorland. Lleu rode behind me as he had the first day, but now I gave him no support or help. He kept himself upright in the saddle through sheer strength of will, riding doggedly, dazed with weariness.

Before dark we came upon a small, round hill, wider and lower than the mounds we had passed earlier. Here we dismounted. Lleu did not resist when I laid my hands on his shoulders to rub gently at the tense muscles across the back of his neck. "Will we stop here?" Agravain asked. At the bottom of the slope the rise of land cut off some of the wind, though it was still cold and could not compare to the protection the forest had offered us.

"Climb," I said. "There's better shelter back of this ridge."

Agravain led the horses, and I guided Lleu the little way to the top. The mound was not a hill but an earthen rampart around a bowl-shaped trough. The outer ridge formed a wall about the hollow of the hill, and sheltered there an ancient ring of stones. Those that were fallen now squatted balefully, but a few still stood upright or pointed at drunken angles to the sky. Lleu stood shivering beneath my hands at the top of the ridge, staring at this old and forgotten shrine. He murmured, with something like despair in his voice, "We are to shelter here?"

"The earthworks cut off the wind," I said.

"I think I would rather freeze."

Agravain gazed at Lleu with amused derision. "They're only stones," he said. "You're not going to be sacrificed."

"No." Lleu shook himself free of my light hold and said, "How far are we from the road?"

The road was less than a mile south of the circle, but I would not let him know this. "Close by," I answered. "We will reach it tomorrow."

"How close?" he pressed.

"I will not tell you," I answered directly. "You have won this much, this far; but I will give you neither bearing nor hope."

We set camp beneath one of the angled stones. The air was very still. There was no wood for a fire and only the lanterns for light. Lleu took charge of these, appropriating all our steel and flint. He put out the lights but for one, which he set close by him. He kept a hand on the grated lid of a dark lantern, lightly drumming his fingers against it. I could not imagine how he would drive himself through the night.

"He must try to sleep a little," I said quietly to Agravain. "If you and I rest in turns, one of us should be able to take him at last."

But that night was almost as hard for me as it was for Lleu. My cough had grown deep and harsh; it hurt me to swallow, and sometimes even to breathe. Once, when Agravain woke me from a fitful sleep to take my turn at watching Lleu, I struck his hand aside storming, "Don't touch me!"

Agravain muttered with distaste, "I wouldn't. I'm not your mother."

That brought me full awake. I said maliciously, "How you envy me!"

Agravain answered with the fierce devotion that had driven him to serve you at the start. "I do. And I envy the Bright One, for I know how she'll use him once he is under her sway."

Lleu glanced up in undisguised horror. *"What does she want of me?"* He ground his hands into his eyes and leaned back against the old stone, pale and miserable. "Ah, God, you are both damned."

"And you with us," Agravain murmured bitterly.

"No, my soul is my own responsibility," Lleu replied, equally acid, glaring at me. "I have not sold it yet."

I heard in his clear voice an echo of your impatience, an echo of your disdain. Lleu gazed at me and Agravain, where the two of us crouched stiff and shivering in the shadow of the dark rock. "You hope to catch me unaware. I swear you will not do it."

In abrupt, unchecked anger, Agravain dealt his cousin so fierce a blow that Lleu fell sprawling in the snow, stunned. He pressed one hand to his face even as with the other he drew his hunting knife, an easier and less exacting defense than his bow. I uttered in a terrible voice, "Agravain!"

I was so suddenly despising of his blind and adoring obedience to you, and so jealous of my brother's strength of spirit, that I ignored Lleu's disadvantage. What reason had Agravain to hate Lleu, other than that you desired he should?

"Any hurt you deal the prince," I said in quiet fury, "I

172

will deal to you." I struck Agravain carelessly across the face. He stared at me in astonished resentment. "Do you understand that?" I asked in the same voice.

"Yes, sir," he muttered.

"Perfect," I said, "Don't hit him again."

Lleu moved back to his place by the lantern, certain of the knife he held, and sure of nothing else. "What game do you play now? Whose side are you on?" he demanded angrily of me.

"You must think that I answer to the queen of the Orcades as a dog answers to its master," I said bitterly. "But I will not see you harmed without reason."

"You have threatened to kill me!" Lleu protested.

"There is reason for that," I answered.

In the morning we came to the straight, paved Roman road that runs directly to Ratae Coritanorum. It was barely recognizable beneath the snow; around us the moorland was desolate as ever. Lleu gave a little sigh, trying to conceal his relief. But Agravain guided the horses to turn south along the road. Lleu shook his head. "What are you doing?"

"I am leaving you," Agravain explained with elaborate precision. "My mother is waiting for me, and I am taking the horses and continuing south. On foot it will take you two days to reach Camlan."

"All right," said Lleu. "I will seek shelter and rest in Aquae Arnemetiae; it cannot be more than seven or eight miles north of here." He turned as though to walk away, but I laid one hand lightly on his shoulder and said, "I will join you."

"Sir?" Agravain questioned stonily. "You will not come with me?"

"What for?" I sneered. "It is no triumph to return from the hunt without having made a kill. I have no desire to journey to Ratae Coritanorum without the required trophy."

"What am I to tell the queen?" Agravain cried harshly. "Why would you come so far in such a venture and then turn back?"

"But I am not turning back," I answered, "merely aside, to follow my own will."

"Wait," Lleu interrupted. "What do you mean? You can't be following your own will if you take the road with me."

"I can. I can ransom you myself."

He glanced at my hand lightly resting on his shoulder, his expression agonized. "You would kill me yourself, if my father refused your demands?"

"I would," I said quietly.

"I am still free."

I took his face between my hands. He did not try to turn away, but regarded me through dark, desolate eyes ringed with smudges of blue shadow. "Yes. You are still free," I repeated in quiet.

"Come with me, then, I don't care," he said with reckless, passionate courage. "I would rather die by your hand, I would rather have my death prey at your heart forever, than be instantly forgotten by your heartless mother."

"You must understand how defenseless you have left yourself," I whispered. It was chilling to hear him speak so bluntly of his own death, he who was afraid of the dark.

"I understand," Lleu said with bleak clarity. "We are alone, and it is dead of winter; and only by my own faltering strength can I keep from falling prisoner to you. When finally I fail I will be yours, hated and envied, for you to use as you will. So I wait on your fury."

"Brilliant," I said. "Agravain, here we leave you."

"How dare you!" Agravain said. He seemed suddenly as young as Lleu, and as desperate, about to be left alone in the wilderness in an unfamiliar land.

"I dare because I have drunk my fill of the queen of the Orcades," I said vehemently. "You can go back to your mother and you can tell her that I am no longer her ward. Tell her that I owe her nothing. Tell her that my treachery is of my own making. She drew me in and now I am up to my neck in it, but I am in it for myself and not as her minion." I went to the horses, untied certain of the satchels and slung them over my shoulders, and then tied blankets and furs together in a bundle that I could carry on my back. "Take the horses, Agravain. We'll walk."

I took Lleu by the elbow and started up the road through the snow, leaving Agravain staring after us in puzzlement and anger. Now I was alone in the wasteland with my young brother, and we walked slowly north toward the higher hills; or toward home, or toward death, into the wind.

XIII
Aquae Arnemetiae

Lleu and I walked without speaking, as we had for the last three days; except now our silence was mutual, shared, something that did not separate us but rather bound us together. The oppressive cold and silence never abated. Only the old road that we followed made the landscape different. Now and then the roof of a cottage or shepherd's hut appeared huddled under the shadow of a low hill, or a stone wall marked off the boundary of a snow-covered field. Otherwise the barren white wasteland about us remained unaltered, the monotony of the moor unbroken.

But once Lleu stopped, astonished, staring at the blank road before him. He blinked and put a hand to his temple. "What was that?" he said.

I watched him, intrigued. "What do you think it was?" There had been no sound, no movement, no sudden shaft of sunlight.

"I thought—" He frowned, rubbing at his forehead. "It was a flash of color, across the road—a bird or butterfly, green and gold and scarlet. But it's gone. . . ." He hesitated, hearing the madness in his words. "You didn't see."

"No." I touched his shoulder lightly to set him walking again.

We traveled seven or eight miles without stopping to rest. In the early afternoon the road led us down into a valley, to what had been the Roman city of Aquae Arnemetiae, a city of healing pools and mineral wells. The Roman baths lay crumbling into ruin now; the springs were beginning to break free of the shrines that had been built around them, though they ran clear and warm as they always had. The outer buildings of the old city lay as rubble, roofless and empty. But the heart of the town remained inhabited. On one of the streets that we passed through there was a public house with its door open, and from within, fragments of quiet conversation echoed in the street. I unslung the small bleak leather satchel that I carried and put a hand in, searching for the few coins I had brought with me. I said to Lleu, "Shall we eat here?"

He watched in horror and amazement as I drew my hand out of the bag. I saw the fear in his look, but could not understand it. Disturbed and puzzled, I said, "What is it? You can't be afraid to take a meal among other people."

Lleu whispered, "Why do you carry feathers in your bag?"

"Feathers?" I asked, speaking low, and feeling curiously fearful myself. "Feathers . . . ," I repeated slowly. "Where did you see them?"

We stood beneath the eaves of the low building, talking in quiet voices, as would any two traveling companions who might pass through the town and debate whether or not to take their midday meal in company of the townsmen.

"You shook them out of your satchel just now," Lleu said. "Didn't you? A handful of black feathers, like snowflakes of shadow, they fluttered from your fingers and scattered across the street—"

"Ai, God help you, Lleu," I whispered. I stood a moment considering whether he had any idea of what was happening. Then I bent and reached down as though picking up some small thing near my boot, and held my hand before his face. "A feather like this one?"

"There's nothing there," Lleu said.

"Are you sure?" I slowly turned my hand.

His face betrayed him. "What did you see?" I asked.

"I don't know," Lleu gasped quietly. "You're not—holding anything."

"No," I said. "I'm not. But you saw something."

We both stood still and silent. Lleu looked at the white doves in the eaves of the building across the street, then closed his eyes with a small cry and quickly turned his face away.

"Come, let's eat here," I said. "You must rest, Lleu. You will destroy yourself if you go on like this."

Lleu said carefully, "Suppose the folk in this place have heard that I have been abducted?"

"That is a risk I take."

"And if I cry to them for sanctuary?"

"Will you?" I asked.

"No," he said. "This is our contest now, yours and mine alone. I will not force my father's people to choose between us."

We stepped inside the small, dark shop. There were a dozen or so men there, shepherds and farmers from the nearby moors, and a few townsmen. I asked for bowls of porridge and mugs of warm ale for myself and Lleu, and the other patrons made room for us on one of the benches. Lleu looked up from his food to scan the faces around him, as though one might prove to be compassionate or even familiar; but he suddenly sank his face against his forearm, leaning on the table, his shoulders shaking. "Sit up, you little idiot," I said in his ear, helping him to straighten. "What's the matter?"

"I thought one of the men was horned with stag's antlers, like the lord of death and the Wild Hunt," Lleu whispered despairingly. "Oh, God, I am so tired." When he finally gathered the courage to pick up his mug his hands shook so much that he spilled a good deal on the table. The men sitting near threw him curious glances, but decently looked away when they saw me gently take the cup from Lleu's hands and wipe the table.

When I went to pay for our meal the keeper of the hostel remarked quietly to me, "It's a bad time to travel far in open country. Is the boy simple?"

Lleu heard, and flung up his head in defiance, but he said nothing. I answered, "He's not simple. A bit of a fool, perhaps." I beckoned Lleu with a nod of my head. "He could shape entertainment in a king's court, couldn't you, little one?" I said. "Give them the performance we had at Midwinter's."

"You dare tempt me!" Lleu said aloud. He rose to stand before me and handed his bow and quiver to one of the patrons. Then in spite of his exhaustion, in spite of the tricks his eyes were playing him, in the small space between a table and a screen of woven rush he executed two fast, furious handsprings, forward and backward. Afterward he clung to the nearest table for support, blinking to clear his unreliable vision, as the astonished patrons burst into a roar of approval and admiration.

"Hey, Maria," the proprietor called into the inner room, pushing aside the wattled reeds. "Bring the children out here. There's an acrobat."

A thin woman came out of the back room, dogged by two small boys; the elder looked about six years old, and the other, whose face and hands were covered with flour, was perhaps two years younger. The little one hid behind his mother's skirts, peering out through his dusty fingers. "Come on, you lot," the owner directed. "Stand back, clear some room."

They dragged the tables and benches aside and waited expectantly, all gazing at Lleu. He glanced around the dark room, biting his lip; then suddenly he laughed and ran a hand through his hair, and spoke in his clear, authoritative voice:

"Under your green-girt beams I come
Neither to beg nor borrow;
Instead I play upon your hearth
To speed away all sorrow.
I am the sun lord's namesake—
Cry welcome to me here!
Fortune I bring to field and fold
At the closing of the year."

He looked at me and grinned and shrugged, while his small audience applauded and called encouragement. He turned a few more elegant handsprings, and the children watched with round eyes. Lleu suddenly knelt by the older boy and said, "Would you like to try?"

The child nodded. Lleu stood and led his pupil to the center of the floor, then holding the small hands flipped the boy head over heels two or three times, back and forth. The child laughed in delight, until at last Lleu set him down. "Such talent!" he praised. He ruffled the boy's hair and added, "I could teach you to use a sword, as well. But perhaps that is enough for today."

"One more stunt, then?" someone called. Lleu obligingly stood on one hand for a good half a minute before he flipped himself to his feet. Finally he breathed deeply and bowed, and moved to stand at my side.

The men cheered and applauded and thumped their fists against the tables, and the hostel's keeper poured another drink for Lleu in payment for his performance.

"My thanks, master," Lleu said as he reached for the cup, grinning still in exhausted pleasure; but instead of drinking he suddenly cried out, "Ah, no!" and threw the mug aside. He buried his face in my sleeve and mumbled incoherently, "The handle moved. I thought it was a snake." I put my arm around his shoulders and stroked the back of his head.

The townsfolk turned their faces away, hushed, and the woman said to the children, "Now away with you." They ran back into the other room.

The proprietor said to me in a low voice, "If I can help him in any way—do you need shelter for the night? You need not pay for it."

Lleu raised his head and answered for both of us, refusing the man's offer with quiet finality. "Thank you, but no. I am very tired, and we have a long way to go."

I loaded the blankets and satchels on my back, then drew Lleu's cloak over his shoulders and fastened it for him. The man who held Lleu's bow offered it up to me; Lleu stood before the little crowd and held out an open hand, his gaze demanding. I surrendered the bow to him.

The other patrons moved aside so that we had a clear path to the door. As Lleu passed by the thin, tired-looking woman, she took his hand and held it to her lips in formal respect. She said quietly, "God go with you, fair one."

It cut at my heart mercilessly. What need had he to be any kind of warrior or administrator? He was instantly beloved of his people; all he must do is turn a somersault and pet a child, and he has won them to him body and soul.

"Why did you not accept that offer?" I asked him as we left the city, following the road uphill and northward.

"Because you are with me," Lleu answered bitterly. He spoke as he walked, plowing through the snow with his head down, watching his feet. "Because they looked to you as my protector, my guide. You could see they thought me out of my senses; if I had fought to resist you they would have fought against me, and all with the best of intentions."

"Perhaps." I halted, and he turned to look at me. I said, "Here we leave the road."

Lleu protested passionately, dreading to return to the forest and uninhabited moorland after the laughter and warmth of the town. "No! Why? Cross the moor yourself! I dare not depend on you to show me the way!"

"You no longer have the strength to take the road alone," I said patiently. "This way is more direct, and will bring us to Camlan sooner."

"Why would you want to get there sooner?"

"Like yourself, I am not in such matchless physical form," I answered.

"True," he sneered. "You've been nursing a raging fever since our first night in the open." A breathless little laugh escaped him. "To think it is you who have taken chill, not I!"

"But I'm not hallucinating," I said softly. "No matter which of us is in control when we reach Camlan, we both need to get there quickly."

Lleu stormed reluctantly in my trail as we walked away from the road. We climbed through the bare forest, and covered several more miles. At dusk we were close to another stretch of empty hilltop, and we stopped among the trees to make camp: this time only a small fire, and the furs and blankets spread next to it. Lleu unpacked the little dried fruit and cheese that was left, and heated wine. At first he would not let me help, but in the midst of his preparations he gasped in wonder, "My hands are bleeding." He held out a hand, palm up, gloveless. "Look: blood running between my fingers, staining my sleeve."

I could scarcely bear to listen to him. "Put your gloves on," I said. His sleeve was unspotted.

After that he let me deal with the food. He avoided touching anything lest it change shape before his eyes.

When we had eaten he took off his cloak and folded it double, and wrapped it around his shoulders that way beneath the blankets and furs in which he huddled. He was nearer the fire than I, yet he was still shivering. I could not imagine being so cold; I could not feel the cold even in my hands. I sang under my breath from the dark story of Lleu's shining namesake:

> "Grows an oak on upland plain,
> Darkly shadowed sky and glen;
> Nine score hardships hath he suffered
> In its top, Lleu Llaw Gyffes."

"Ah, shut it," Lleu said.

"Even now you remind me of your namesake," I said gently. "You can no longer rely on the strength of your own body, the integrity of your own mind. Think of Lleu enchanted, imprisoned in another form! Think how it must be to look at your hands and see an eagle's talons, clawed and cruel."

Lleu interrupted with a wordless cry of horror. He slammed his hands over his ears and said furiously, "That tale ends with order restored and justice done. You know that. Lleu is rescued and healed; his lands are returned to him, and he is revenged."

"And in truth, his punishment seems little worse than the visions you are enduring," I said. I drank some of the wine without heating it, and rubbed a fistful of snow over my forehead. "What makes you shiver so?"

He stared at me with hatred and derision. He sat with his knees drawn up close to his chest, his gloved hands in tight fists beneath his chin. "Come," I said, and held out an arm so that he might sit against my shoulder.

He muttered, "I don't want your cold."

"I offer you my warmth," I said.

Reluctantly, resentfully, he curled himself into the hollow between my arm and chest. I murmured low,

"Grows an oak upon a steep,
The sanctuary of a fair lord;
If I speak not falsely,
Lleu will come into my lap."

Lleu sighed and closed his eyes, but soon forced them open again, mistrusting me. He stared at the fire as it burned lower and lower.

But I was tired beyond endurance in my own right. Before long we were both dozing. I did not have the energy to struggle with Lleu, and let him sink into the deep, sound sleep of utter exhaustion. Finally I folded the blankets around us both and slept also.

I woke because I was cold. The fever had peaked and broken while I slept, and I sat up in the dark, thirsty and chilled. The fire had gone out, but the night was not completely black; the clouds had cleared, and the sky through the bare trees blazed with starlight. The moon was new and had already set. I could see Lleu in the dim light; he slept profoundly with his dark head muffled in the dark leather of his sleeve, vulnerable. Cautiously, quickly, I drew the knife from his belt and cut his bowstring.

But I woke him doing this. Lleu forced his eyes open and propped his head on an elbow, shivering, to sit up suddenly as he realized what had happened. He stayed frozen, apprehensive; then, shifting his weight slowly, he marked where my hand flashed with the glimmer of silver. He leaped at me and in our struggle I dropped the dagger, but caught it by the blade with my other hand.

After a moment of absolute stillness Lleu reached down and seized my wrist. He threw all his weight against my arm, and when he had it pinned beneath him, he forced my stiff fingers shut around the dagger's edge. Then he slowly but firmly wrenched the knife out of my hand—

Ah, God, my hand.

The blade cut through my glove, deep across my palm and the inside of my fingers. I gasped and pulled away from him, overwhelmed.

Lleu said fiercely, "That hurt, didn't it! You're bleeding."

Malevolent, swift, I tore off the glove and dashed my hand across his face.

He cried out in horror and hid his face in his sleeve. Then he drove the knife through the darkness until he held it against my throat. We both were still again, poised like that: I breathing through clenched teeth in short, harsh bursts, Lleu utterly silent. He held the knife there for a few moments, then flung it skittering away into the dark. "I've never killed anyone, any man," he whispered. "I cannot do it."

"You have the skill," I whispered in answer. I pressed my throbbing hand to my side beneath my other arm. "But you need more than skill, do you not?"

Lleu sat dumb. He rubbed his eyes. "I don't hate you," he said stubbornly. "I don't want to kill you."

"Death," I whispered, "often has very little to do with hatred. When hunting one kills through need of food or else for sport and love of skill—never through hatred. When you hate something you do not kill it. You hurt it." The pain in my hand made me mindless, and ruthless, and I was determined to punish him. I rested another moment; then with sudden strength I forced Lleu to the ground and held him there with one arm pinned beneath him and drew my torn hand across his mouth and over his eyelids. Lleu screamed.

My fingers were dripping. Lleu pushed away from me with his free arm, but I caught at him with my sound right hand, and held his gloved fingers so tightly they began to feel stiff. He screamed again, out of sheer desperation.

"Wild thing," I whispered. "I'd like to cut your hands off, burn you, blind you . . . I should crush your slender fingers. I could break all the bones in your hand if I closed my own around yours tightly enough. You are as pure and dangerous as an untamed cat; your beauty makes me sick. And oh, God, you have hurt me, you have hurt me. . . ."

I steadied my voice. "But I am afraid to risk my father's trust in me, or what is left of it. I am afraid to kill you outright. I thought of ruining you in some irreparable way, so that you could never be king, though you'd still be alive and I'd seem blameless. I could deafen you; there's a way to direct blows against your ears that will take away your hearing." Lleu tried to pull his hand away, and my iron hold on his fingers grew even more impossible. "Do you doubt me?" I said. "Or I could half smother you; when you go without air for too long it damages your mind, though it need not kill you. And there are things I can do to punish you that you will find more dreadful than any hurt. Be still." I bent over, my wounded hand in his hair, and pressing my mouth to Lleu's warm, windburned lips, kissed him gently.

He lay rigid, as though he had been scalded.

"Your mouth is sweet," I said.

"*God,*" Lleu breathed. His hair was cold. He smelled of earth and snow and blood.

"Lie still," I said. "Lie still. Am I not well armed against you even without steel? I need no more than a few drops of blood, and this. . . ."

"Don't," Lleu said quietly. "Don't, my lord."

He spoke without fear. In his voice I heard only authority and reproach. It was as though he meant to remind me how very much I had to lose.

He struggled again to escape my grip, but I held him fast. "What do you want, Medraut? The inheritance you would win from our father will never give you power over me, *me;* and I will never beg for your mercy, even though you try to drive me mad. I may be afraid of death, but I do not fear *you.*"

"So you say," I spat.

He winced and turned his face away. "Then do what you will with me," he choked. "You are just like your mother. You would gently ruin me if it served your ends; and in revengeful punishment you hurt and hurt and hurt. I wounded you in self-defense, I did not mean to do it! If I must pay for that with my sight, then put my eyes out! Is that just? Is that fair? Hurting me will not heal your hand, or make me regret that I tried to save myself. By that law you should have been buried alive for your mistake in the mines at Elder Field."

"You are right," I said slowly, letting go of him and struggling to my knees. "But you have never been held accountable for anything you have ever done."

He sat up also, savagely wiping his mouth, and began to say, "You throw this in my face as though—"

"No," I interrupted. "I mean, you are going to atone for what you have done to me now. You are going to stitch shut my hand."

"I am not!" he cried.

"By God, you are," I said fiercely. I had grown accustomed to the dark, and I could see the strip of white linen at Lleu's wrist, and beyond my reach the silver gleam of the brooch that should clasp his cloak. I felt for the cloak and bound it around my hand, trying to stanch the bleeding. It would not stop. "Now, damn you: there. There by the fire, the lantern's lying there." I prodded him in the right direction. "I don't know what you've done with the flint and tinder, but there's needle and thread in the black leather bag. You must pass the needle through a flame first, to cleanse it. And you'll have to clean the cut, too; you can use snow for that."

"Do it yourself," Lleu said desperately.

I answered with equal desperation, *"I can't."*

He found the lantern and set about lighting it with trembling hands. He dropped the flint in the dead fire at first and had to search for it in the hot, feathery, gray ashes; but at last he was rewarded with the scratch and spurt of a tiny new flame, and he lit the candle in the little lantern and opened the grated door so that as much light as possible spilled from it. I sat bent over my hand, and glanced up at Lleu impassively. "Ah, little brother, don't cry."

Lleu rubbed his eyes angrily. "I'm not. It's the light."

"There's blood on your face," I said. "And in your hair, too, it looks."

"I don't care," Lleu said, and went to collect clean snow.

Eventually he held my torn palm between his hands, needle at ready. He breathed deeply for a few moments but did not move, apparently lacking the courage to begin the operation. Again I underestimated him. Without warning he stabbed viciously at the deep slash across my palm.

I yelped in surprise and pain and snatched my hand away. Lleu said credulously, "I thought you couldn't feel anything in those fingers."

"You cretin," I gasped. "Give me the needle, I'll do it myself."

"I'll do it, Medraut," he said quietly. "I'll do it. But I will not let you take me." This time he bent to the work with patience and gentleness. And it was bitterly cold.

XIV
The Year's Turning

Lleu took a long time, for he worked meticulously and carefully. When it was over we sat in the gray predawn in silence, both of us drained beyond speaking, or even moving. At last Lleu bandaged my hand and then began to gather and fold the blankets. When he had done I rekindled the fire and heated the last of the wine for us to drink with what was left of the dried fruit and bread. While I worked, Lleu sat by the fire with his face in his hands, and when I offered him food he shook his head.

The morning was cold and clear, breathtaking, brilliant. The splendor of the sun was almost unbearable after so many continuous clouded days. The brightness of it seemed to hurt Lleu; he winced, squinting, when he finally raised his face from his hands, and for a long time he kept a shielding hand over his eyes. He could not stop shivering. But when I held his cloak to him he shuddered and said, "Burn it." It was filthy with my blood. I tossed the cloak on the dying fire and then threw the blankets on top of it. They smoked and smoldered, disintegrating.

We set out once more through light, powdery snow and trees with branches sparkling where icicles were forming in the sunlight. We crossed into moorland and began to journey downhill. We walked miles without speaking, left the high moor and once more traveled through forest. But it was a different forest than the one we had left behind; here the trees were taller and farther apart. Lleu did not notice. After his scant few hours of sleep he no longer hallucinated, but he could scarcely keep his feet. He stumbled more and more often, and finally he stopped walking altogether. He stood motionless and waited for me to face him.

I turned toward him when he halted. The fury and tension of the night still hung between us like a thunderhead. I knew that he had reached the end of his strength and that only a little resistance on my part would make him mine. I broke an icicle from a frozen branch to use as a weapon and dragged it across his cheek.

He stood still and closed his eyes, but did not attempt to reach for the knives at his waist. I ran the ice over his throat, sharp as a hunting knife and even colder, held the crystalline blade beneath his chin and watched the reflected sunlight dancing there. "Even now you seem undefeated," I whispered, "and though I might take you easily I do not really want your inheritance. It is your self, your soul, that I envy. More than anything I want your birthright without shame, your clean lineage."

"You can never have that," Lleu said, with his eyes closed and his head held still; though one of his hands had flown to his ashen face, almost accidentally, guarding his eyes. "How can anyone change that?"

I trailed the ice across his gloved palm, then took him by the wrist and eased his arm back down. Lleu opened his eyes cautiously, dazzled by sunlight and the sparkling ice so close to his face. "I cannot change it," I admitted, "but with you at my mercy I can make my father acknowledge that the fault was his. That I am no more a creature of my mother's making than he is."

"Not her creature!" Lleu burst out. "Why else would you ransom my life to solace your own bruised pride? No one cares who your parents were! People admire you or despise you for yourself, for what you have made yourself. What have I to do with it? You do not envy my parentage, you envy me."

I stood gazing at him without any answer to give, feeling myself to be so base, so wrong, so ruined. My fingers were locked around his wrist as surely as steel. He said half wondering, "Ai, my brother, you are so strong and light in form, so wise and deft in mind, so gentle and true in semblance . . ."

"So ruthlessly cruel in truth," I finished, whispering.

Now tears began to glitter cold and hopeless across his face.

I turned his hand over and broke the brittle ice easily across his palm. There was hardly anything for him to feel: a touch of chill through his glove, then shattered crystals melting to nothing on his open hand. "It's only water, Lleu," I said quietly. "If I held such a thing to your sunlit face for much longer than two moments it would dissolve into air." I brushed my fingertips across his cheek and smeared the tears there. He sank to his knees in the snow. The sunlight was cold through the bare trees, and the ground was frozen and desolate. "Lleu," I said softly, and reached for his hands to help him back to his feet.

"I can't," he whispered. "I can't, I can't."

I knelt beside him. "Lleu, get up. You've no cloak. You'll freeze."

"You're going to kill me, anyway," he whispered, too tired to raise his voice.

I shook my head, speechless, desperate with remorse and self-hatred. He did not notice. Holding him steady with one hand, I undid the clasp at my shoulder and took off my cloak, spreading its soft folds over my knees and the bright snow around us. I drew him close; and too frozen and exhausted to object, Lleu collapsed onto the warm wool and leaned against my chest, folded in my arms. He began to cry in earnest, sobbing with his face buried in my jacket, then crying uncontrollably in breathless, shrieking gasps that tore through his entire body. "Don't," I whispered. "Don't."

When his sobs began to sound less like screams I rested one cheek against his hair and bent over him, cradling him like a child. He clutched at my jacket with cold, clenched, tear-wet fingers. I laughed a little. "You cling to me so—do you still trust me, after all this?"

He said in a low, broken voice, "I have always trusted you."

Then of a sudden he stopped crying. He twisted around in my arms so that he could see me. "If you would kill me," he said, "kill me now."

Having said that, his voice grew stronger. "Do it. Do it! Stab me and leave my body to whatever creatures roam this wood, and no one will ever know. No one will ever blame you."

I whispered, "I could not butcher you."

He was guessing, daring, with his life forfeit if he were wrong. But he knew he was right. "Then leave me here," he said. "I can't walk. I don't know where I am. I would be dead of cold by evening, and again you could escape blame." He choked, half weeping still, and burst forth, "I am your brother! You are my friend! You are the single person I have most admired and imitated and envied my entire life! If you hate me so for my heritage, then I do not want it, I cannot bear your hatred. So leave me here! Kill me!"

"I can't," I gasped. "I can't. I can't kill you. I love you."

You see what it took to make me know this.

I held Lleu fiercely, shaking, my face turned away, and lashed myself with degrading epithets: serpent, seducer, defiling deceiver, corrupted outcast, traitor and toad. But to revile myself did nothing to help Lleu. He sobbed a while longer, frustrated in his exhaustion, though he had triumphed over me in a way he could never have planned. His unconditional trust and love were prizes I never knew I coveted, infinitely more powerful and more healing than the fear I had tried to exact from him. He whispered at last, yawning, "You are not evil, but you are so torn! What drives you? If I became high king you'd have more power than any man in Britain, but you choose to follow Morgause."

"She taught me all I know of cruelty, that's true," I said. "But Lleu, you brought on the fury that drove me to attempt such a thing. When you're unwilling to do as your father tells you, does he invoke his power as high king and say that it is not within your right to disobey him?"

"Do I do that?"

"You have told me I have not so much as the right to object if you choose to insult me! Even the queen of the Orcades grants me that!"

"That was childish of me. I tried to apologize."

I sighed. "I know you did. But I had my mother's hatred to strengthen my own. Now she has made me hate myself more than I ever hated you. I will be free."

Lleu sighed and closed his eyes. "Maybe you will. But she still triumphs. I'll die anyway; I have no strength to make the journey home."

Anguished to hear him speak so, I said gently, "We're barely five miles from Camlan. Did you really not know that?"

He bit his lip. He had seen without fear that he might be dying, and it must be hard now to learn how close he was to home. "You'll have to leave me," he said. "I can't walk any farther."

"You're not afraid?"

"Not since I know you won't slay me."

I whispered, "If you die now, I will have slain you." I wrapped my cloak around his shoulders. "I'll carry you."

"Sir, how can you?" Lleu also whispered. "I am almost as tall as you."

"I will," I said. "Damn her! I won't be used any longer!" The emotions I had fought so long to deny fired my vehemence. "You've driven yourself almost to madness in defiance of my cruelty and I'll find the strength to carry you home if it leaves me broken forever."

Without a further word I gathered Lleu in my arms and

staggered to my feet. "Five miles?" Lleu whispered. "Oh, sir . . . your hand, and the fever . . ."

"What are they measured against your life?" I cried. "The fever has passed. The hand's already ruined." I shifted his weight more comfortably in my arms and slowly began to walk westward beneath the trees. "Try to sleep now," I added. Lleu leaned his head against my shoulder and slept.

After only a little way I had to stop and rest in exhaustion. I cannot do this, I thought despairingly, it is like trying to carry a young buck in my arms. Idiot, I cursed myself then; you who call yourself a huntsman, would you carry a buck in your arms? After that I slung him over my shoulders. He hardly noticed. He slept as deeply as if he had been drugged.

Not long before dark I was arrested by the sound of a horse behind us, out of sight among the trees but coming closer at a gallop. I had no time to prepare myself against this unknown rider, no time to wake Lleu enough that he could be set on his feet. I turned to face whatever was coming, standing with straight defiance, for all that I bore Lleu on my back. I would not let myself consider how spent I was. I stood waiting, watching the rider arrive in a storm of flying hooves and snow.

It was Goewin. She must have known she was coming upon me even before she had seen me; she sat her horse with a spear balanced under one arm, as if she were leading an army into battle. She pulled her horse to a sudden and startling halt, sending up another burst of flying snow. Clumps of it settled in my hair, and in the folds of the cloak wrapped about Lleu.

"We saw your smoke," she said. "The blankets you left smoldering there made a cloud black as a tunnel. Did you think no one would notice? What a place to light a fire, if you were trying to go unseen! Another half mile and you'd have been at the summit of Shining Ridge, where the beacons are lit." She spoke in hard, clean anger, controlled.

"What makes you sure I meant to go unseen?" I said faintly.

"Agravain said you planned to kill the prince yourself," Goewin said, with no trace of fear in her voice, though Lleu hung still and pale over my shoulders. "I do not trust Agravain so far as I can push him, but you have betrayed my trust as well. You could—you could have at any time—arranged Lleu's death so that it looked like accident, or someone else's fault." Still she covered her fear. "Have you?"

"No," I said. "He sleeps only." I said then, "Agravain? Agravain returned to Camlan?"

"He arrived early this morning," Goewin answered. "He feared his mother's wrath more than the king's. And he told us all." Her hard, clear voice never faltered or changed pitch. She gazed down at me with imperious cold dark eyes. "We went out searching when he arrived, I and my father and Caius. We were going to make Agravain take us back to the place where he left you, but we saw your smoke and found your camp. You tell me, my lord brother, what we were to think: shreds of Lleu's cloak crumbling to ashes in that stinking, smoking pile of debris, blood in the snow, our satchels and bags abandoned there."

"The blood was mine," I said, shifting Lleu's weight. "You see." I held my bandaged hand away from his body.

The air rang with hoofbeats as Goewin's companions caught up with her. "Hai!" she called to them, raising her spear as a standard. "They are here." Artos and Caius rode into our company, with Agravain between them. "Lleu!" Artos cried, swinging down from his horse, and Caius leveled a spear at me.

"He's alive," Goewin said coldly. "Stand back." Not one of them, not the high king himself, stepped forward to disobey her command.

"Well, Medraut, there were two sets of footprints," Goewin said. "We knew you had not killed him. We followed to where the snow was marked as though someone had lain there, and after that there were only your prints. I could not think what you had done to Lleu, though I knew you must be carrying him—there was no blood, no body."

She had led them here. She was still their leader.

Her voice was calm, but she spoke through clenched teeth. "What have you done to him?"

It was I who faltered. I opened my mouth to speak, hesitated, and managed at last to whisper hoarsely, "I won't say. I can't tell you."

She slid from her horse, her spear tilted at me. "You can't tell me—can he? Will he? Dear God! I should—" Of a sudden she hit me furiously across my shins with the butt of her spear. I staggered abruptly to my knees.

Artos stepped forward and put a cautionary hand on Goewin's shoulder, but gave no word of reprimand. I clung to Lleu, who raised his head wearily, awakened by the sudden jolt.

199

"Put him down," Goewin said. Lleu stared at her and at his father, unbelieving, used to being tricked by what he saw. "Put him down!" Goewin cried again, her spear threatening. I gently set Lleu on his feet. He stood next to me a moment, balancing himself with one unsteady hand lightly resting on my shoulder; then he carefully crossed to stand beside his father. I faced Goewin, on my knees in the snow before her.

"You—you don't even obey your precious mother!" Goewin said. "Whom do you serve—yourself? Some forgotten god of darkness?" And then with the staff of her spear she struck a tremendous blow to the side of my head. I reeled, falling sideways into the snow with all my weight against my wounded hand, and could not stifle a sharp cry of real pain. I said nothing, only raised my head a little to watch for the next attack; neither defiant nor afraid, resigned, fully aware of what she meant to do. But when Goewin drew back for another blow Lleu said suddenly, "Don't."

I turned my gaze on Lleu, wondering.

"He hasn't hurt me," Lleu said.

"He might yet," Goewin said coldly.

"He won't," Lleu said. "You will kill him if you go on. There will be nothing won, nothing gained. You'll break yourself, you'll break us all, just as Morgause would have it. Oh, don't be an idiot, Goewin, he is no traitor."

"Oh, is he not!"

Lleu said calmly, "I am safe, I am whole: Don't destroy me now."

"Are you so bound to him?" Goewin sneered. "As he is to his mother?"

"I am not bound to anyone," Lleu said readily. "But he is, after all, our brother."

"Ai, Bright One," Artos said. He took the boy by the shoulders so that they could see one another and then embraced him: they stood trembling in each other's arms, both of them close to tears. Artos said, "He has changed you. He has done it."

"Oh, God, no," I said passionately. "I only tried to hurt him. He changed himself. He changed *me*."

I sat in the snow, waiting. Lleu stood beneath his father's heavy, loving hands, and said, "Ask again who it is that Medraut follows."

Goewin asked without speaking, with her eyes and a small, questioning shrug.

I drew myself up onto one knee, my head held proudly, and whispered in honesty and pain: "I serve the prince of Britain." And in a stronger voice I added, "The Bright One. Lleu son of Artos.

"My lord, my brother, I have hated and envied you. . . ." Then my voice broke, and I could no longer speak formally. "Ah, Goewin, finish me if you must, I am sick to death of being feared and mistrusted."

She looked at me and then at Lleu. Lleu's face was impassive but set; his look was one of authority and fairness, adult and certain. "All right!" she said quietly, and threw down her spear. "All right."

"Come, my marksman," Artos said, my father also, forbidding and forgiving. He stepped forward to take my hands and raised me to my feet. "I told you once that you could always come back to me."

That is why I cannot come back to you, Godmother.

Lleu sighed, shuddering with exhaustion and relief. Then he suddenly and softly laughed aloud, quietly but with elation. He covered his eyes with one hand, as though he thought his laughter inappropriate; the joy in his half-hidden smile struck me like oblique sunlight.

"Lleu—," Goewin began in concern.

"I am so glad," he said clearly, unmasking his radiant face as he turned to look at her, "that this is finished."

That is why I will never come back to you.

Artos helped Lleu to Goewin's horse, then mounted his own. Goewin and I went on foot, one of us on either side of Lleu, taking care that he did not fall. We turned westward toward the fading light. In the gathering dusk the sky still glowed rose on the horizon; soon we left the wood and could see at last the trees of the Edge, black and perfect against the sky. Below, the lights of Camlan flickered and beckoned in the near distance. We finished the journey home across that broad, bright country.

So the new year began.

BUILDING A NEW FANTASY TRADITION

The Unlikely Ones by Mary Brown
Anne McCaffrey raved over *The Unlikely Ones*: "What a splendid, unusual and intriguing fantasy quest! You've got a winner here. . . ." Marion Zimmer Bradley called it "Really wonderful . . . I shall read and re-read this one." A traditional quest fantasy with quite an unconventional twist, we think you'll like it just as much as Anne McCaffrey and Marion Zimmer Bradley did.

Knight of Ghosts and Shadows
by Mercedes Lackey & Ellen Guon
Elves in L.A.? It would explain a lot, wouldn't it? In fact, half a millennium ago, when the elves were driven from Europe they came to—where else? —Southern California. Happy at first, they fell on hard times after one of their number tried to force the rest to be his vassals. Now it's up to one poor human to save them if he can. A knight in shining armor he's not, but he's one hell of a bard!

The Interior Life by Katherine Blake
Sue had three kids, one husband, a lovely home and a boring life. Sometimes, she just wanted to escape, to get out of her mundane world and *live* a little. So she did. And discovered that an active fantasy life can be a very dangerous thing—and very real. . . . Poul Anderson thought *The Interior Life* was "a breath of fresh air, bearing originality, exciting narrative, vividly realized characters—everything we have been waiting for for too long."

The Shadow Gate by Margaret Ball
The only good elf is a dead elf—or so the militant order of Durandine monks thought. And they planned on making sure that all the elves in their world (where an elvish Eleanor of Aquitaine ruled in Southern France) were very, very good. The elves of Three Realms have one last spell to bring help . . . and received it: in the form of the staff of the New Age Psychic Research Center of Austin, Texas. . . .

Hawk's Flight by Carol Chase
Taverik, a young merchant, just wanted to be left alone to make an honest living. Small chance of that though: after their caravan is ambushed Taverik discovers that his best friend Marko is the last living descendant of the ancient Vos dynasty. The man who murdered Marko's parents still wants to wipe the slate clean—with Marko's blood. They try running away, but Taverik and Marko realize that there is a fate worse than death . . . That sooner or later, you have to stand and fight.

A Bad Spell in Yurt by C. Dale Brittain
As a student in the wizards' college, young Daimbert had shown a distinct flair for getting himself in trouble. Now the newly appointed Royal Wizard to the backwater Kingdom of Yurt learns that his employer has been put under a fatal spell. Daimbert begins to realize that finding out who is responsible may require all the magic he'd never quite learned properly in the first place—with the kingdom's welfare and his life the price of failure. Good thing Daimbert knows how to improvise!

MERCEDES LACKEY

The Hottest Fantasy Writer Today!

URBAN FANTASY

Knight of Ghosts and Shadows with Ellen Guon
Elves in L.A.? It would explain a lot, wouldn't it? Eric Banyon really needed a good cause to get his life in gear—now he's got one. With an elven prince he must raise an army to fight against the evil elf lord who seeks to conquer all of California.

Summoned to Tourney with Ellen Guon
Elves in San Francisco? Where else would an elf go when L.A. got too hot? All is well there with our elf-lord, his human companion and the mage who brought them all together—until it turns out that San Francisco is doomed to fall off the face of the continent.

Born to Run with Larry Dixon
There are elves out there. And more are coming. But even elves need money to survive in the "real" world. The good elves in South Carolina, intrigued by the thrills of stock car racing, are manufacturing new, light-weight engines (with, incidentally, very little "cold" iron); the bad elves run a kiddie-porn and snuff-film ring, with occasional forays into drugs. *Children in Peril—Elves to the Rescue.* (Book I of the SERRAted Edge series.)

Wheels of Fire with Mark Shepherd
Book II of the SERRAted Edge series.

When the Bough Breaks with Holly Lisle
Book III of the SERRAted Edge series.

HIGH FANTASY
Bardic Voices: The Lark & The Wren
Rune could be one of the greatest bards of her world,
but the daughter of a tavern wench can't get much in the
way of formal training. So one night she goes up to play
for the Ghost of Skull Hill. She'll either fiddle till dawn to
prove her skill as a bard—or die trying. . . .

The Robin and the Kestrel: Bardic Voices II
After the affairs recounted in *The Lark and The Wren*,
Robin, a gypsy lass and bard, and Kestrel, semi-fugitive
heir to a throne he does not want, have married their
fortunes together and travel the open road, seeking their
happiness where they may find it. This is their story. It
is also the story of the Ghost of Skull Hill. Together, the
Robin, the Kestrel, and the Ghost will foil a plot to drive
all music forever from the land. . . .

Bardic Choices: A Cast of Corbies with Josepha Sherman

If I Pay Thee Not in Gold with Piers Anthony
A new hardcover quest fantasy, co-written by the creator
of the "Xanth" series. A marvelous adult fantasy that
examines the war between the sexes and the ethics of
desire! Watch out for bad puns!

BARD'S TALE
Based on the bestselling computer game, *The Bard's
Tale.*™
Castle of Deception with Josepha Sherman
Fortress of Frost and Fire with Ru Emerson
Prison of Souls with Mark Shepherd

Also by Mercedes Lackey:
Reap the Whirlwind with C.J. Cherryh
Part of the Sword of Knowledge series.

The Ship Who Searched with Anne McCaffrey
The Ship Who Sang is not alone!

Wing Commander: Freedom Flight with Ellen Guon
Based on the bestselling computer game, *Wing Commander.*™

Join the Mercedes Lackey national fan club! For information send an SASE (business-size) to Queen's Own, P.O. Box 43143, Upper Montclair, NJ 07043.

Paksenarrion, a simple sheepfarmer's daughter, yearns for a life of adventure and glory, such as the heroes in songs and story. At age seventeen she runs away from home to join a mercenary company, and begins her epic life . . .

ELIZABETH MOON

THE DEED OF PAKSENARRION

"This is the first work of high heroic fantasy I've seen, that has taken the work of Tolkien, assimilated it totally and deeply and absolutely, and produced something altogether new and yet incontestably based on the master. . . . This is the real thing. Worldbuilding in the grand tradition, background thought out to the last detail, by someone who knows absolutely whereof she speaks. . . . Her military knowledge is impressive, her picture of life in a mercenary company most convincing."—**Judith Tarr**

About the author: Elizabeth Moon joined the U.S. Marine Corps in 1968 and completed both Officers Candidate School and Basic School, reaching the rank of 1st Lieutenant during active duty. Her background in military training and discipline imbue The Deed of Paksenarrion *with a gritty realism that is all too rare in most current fantasy.*

"I thoroughly enjoyed *Deed of Paksenarrion*. A most engrossing highly readable work."
—**Anne McCaffrey**

"For once the promises are borne out. *Sheep-farmer's Daughter* is an advance in realism. . . . I can only say that I eagerly await whatever Elizabeth Moon chooses to write next."
—Taras Wolansky, *Lan's Lantern*

*   *   *   *   *

Volume One: Sheepfarmer's Daughter—Paks is trained as a mercenary, blooded, and introduced to the life of a soldier . . . and to the followers of Gird, the soldier's god.

Volume Two: Divided Allegiance—Paks leaves the Duke's company to follow the path of Gird alone—and on her lonely quests encounters the other sentient races of her world.

Volume Three: Oath of Gold—Paks the warrior must learn to live with Paks the human. She undertakes a holy quest for a lost elven prince that brings the gods' wrath down on her and tests her very limits.

*   *   *   *   *

These books are available at your local bookstore, or you can fill out the coupon and return it to Baen Books, at the address below.

SHEEPFARMER'S DAUGHTER • 65416-0 • 506 pp • $4.99 ____
DIVIDED ALLEGIANCE • 69786-2 • 528 pp • $3.95 ____
OATH OF GOLD • 69798-6 • 528 pp • $3.95 ____
or get all three volumes in one special trade paperback edition,
THE DEED OF PAKSENARRION•72104-6•1,040 pp•$15.00 ____

_____

Please send the cover price to: Baen Books, Dept. BA, P.O. Box 1403, Riverdale, NY 10471.

Name_____
Address_____
City_____ State_____ Zip_____

GRAND ADVENTURE
IN GAME-BASED UNIVERSES

With these exciting novels set
in bestselling game universes,
Baen brings you synchronicity at its
best. We believe that familiarity with
either the novel or the game will
intensify enjoyment of the other.
All novels are the only authorized
fiction based on these games and
are published by permission.

THE BARD'S TALE™

Join the Dark Elf Naitachal and his apprentices in
bardic magic as they explore the mysteries of the
world of The Bard's Tale.

Castle of Deception
by Mercedes Lackey & Josepha Sherman
72125-9 * 320 pages * $5.99   _____

Fortress of Frost and Fire
by Mercedes Lackey & Ru Emerson
72162-3 * 304 pages * $5.99   _____

Prison of Souls
by Mercedes Lackey & Mark Shepherd
72193-3 * 352 pages * $5.99   _____

MAGIC AND COMPUTERS DON'T MIX!

RICK COOK

Or . . . do they? That's what Walter "Wiz" Zumwalt is wondering. Just a short time ago, he was a master hacker in a
Silicon Valley office, a very ordinary fellow in a very mundane
world. But magic spells, it seems, are a lot like computer
programs: they're both formulas, recipes for getting things
done. Unfortunately, just like those computer programs, they
can be full of bugs. Now, thanks to a *particularly* buggy spell,
Wiz has been transported to a world of magic—and incredi-
ble peril. The wizard who summoned him is dead, Wiz has
fallen for a red-headed witch who despises him, and no
one—not the elves, not the dwarves, not even the dragons—
can figure out why he's here, or what to do with him. Worse:
the sorcerers of the deadly Black League, rulers of an entire
continent, want Wiz dead—and he doesn't even know why!
Wiz had better figure out the rules of this strange new
world—and fast—or he's not going to live to see Silicon
Valley again.

Here's a refreshing tale from an exciting new writer. It's also a
rarity: a well-drawn fantasy told with all the rigorous logic of
hard science fiction.

69803-6 • 320 pages • $4.99